Praise for 'The Me

'A wonderful story that makes you feel warm inside!'

'The Melting of Miss Angelina Snow was a joy to read. A great warm-hearted romantic comedy with a story that kept me turning the page. I loved it.'
Themah Carrolle-Casey, author of 'A Matter of Time'

'Charming, gently humorous and delightful, Tonia Parronchi's books are a must for lovers of romance who have (just slightly) esoteric leanings'
Valerie Poore, author of 'Watery Ways'

'Unique and Uniquely Beautiful. Tonia Parronchi's "The Melting of Miss Angelina Snow" is one of the most unique and hauntingly beautiful love stories I have ever read. Place and marvellous characters are only two of the reasons to read this romance. The story itself is unique, surprising, and unforgettable. Twists, turns, and spiritual nuances at the core mingle to paint a love story that will drape itself across the canvas of readers' hearts.'
Stephanie Parker McKean, author of 'Bridge to Nowhere'

'Tonia Parronchi is a master at creating living, breathing characters. Those who people this delightful story are not designed, polished and perfect. They are,

instead, the folks who inhabit every person's life on a daily basis. And how does she accomplish that? By being a keen observer of human nature, by creating believable dialogue, by describing the character's flaws, referencing their attributes, and making them human. Then she sets them down in an enchanting story in a picturesque British tableau of seaside villages and one particularly mysterious cave where macabre secrets from the past are still alive awaiting absolution.'
Janet Purcell, author of 'Rooster Street'

Praise for 'The Song of the Cypress

'This is the most lyrical and beautifully written story I have ever read.' Stephanie Parker McKean, author of 'Bridge to Nowhere'

'The Song of the Cypress' is the most beautiful, lyrical book I have read in a very long time. The book reads like poetry; the words ripple like silk across the pages and flow through the book in a gentle, evocative stream'.
Valerie Poore, author of 'Watery Ways'

'Tonia Parronchi has great powers herself, not least a wonderful gift for description. Whatever she describes, she brings to it all a certain enchantment.'
William Wood, author of 'A Little Book of Pleasures'

'I could not put this book down ... It made me yearn to move to the Italian countryside! Tonia has a unique voice, poetic without being cloying, full of humanity and wonderful descriptions.'

'An excellent read, and a magnificent mix of poetry and evocative imagery that intrigued me and keep me wishing for more.'

'I don't recall ever having been so immersed in the flesh and bones of a book as I was in this one and I feel bereft now that I have finished it.'

Praise for 'A Whisper on the Mediterranean

'A Whisper on the Mediterranean' is a more than a book; it is an adventure to be enjoyed on sea or on land, on hot sweltering days or during cold wet evenings. It is a book for everyone, sailor or a land lubber.?'
Michelle Heatley, author of 'Fish Soup'

'Reading your book felt like I was sailing together with you, visiting all those beautiful islands and places. Feeling the wind and the sun, worried about the coming weather. Actually it was more than sailing together, it was like sitting in your head and seeing through your eyes, feeling your emotions. Wonderful reading.'

The Melting of
Miss Angelina Snow

by
Tonia Parronchi

The Melting of Miss Angelina Snow
copyright © by Tonia Parronchi 2017

For Tonino
... and what should have been

Acknowledgements

Once more I need to thank my wonderful family. Guido, whose love and encouragement are so constant. Our son, James and my parents, Audrey and Derek. No one could ask for a better family.

I'd like to thank my friends who are always so supportive of me. In particular my amazing author friends who clarified certain important issues for me, such as 'to comma or not to comma' and other tricky grammatical queries. Val Poore, Stephanie Parker McKean, Janet Purcell and Themah Carrolle-Casey - you are wonderful!

Abby Knight, my fantastic agent, thanks as always for all you do.

Thanks to Steven Novak who designed this book cover and somehow managed to understand exactly what I needed and create the perfect atmosphere with his design.

hanks to Lindsey Dugger - adventuresofalostgirl.com who has done an amazing job recently, updating my website details.

Finally, thanks to my late friend Tonino for inspiring me to write this book as a tribute to him. At the end of this book you can read more about how I came to write this story. I miss you Tony.

1

Dying is Easy

The boatyard was quiet in the late afternoon. Only a few dedicated sailors were spending Sunday preparing their boats for the summer. Leonardo flicked another cigarette butt into the river and drained his brandy glass, refusing to feel guilty at ignoring the doctor's orders. The spring sun felt good on his shoulders. Mina sang slightly-muffled love songs to Celentano on the stereo below deck. Leonardo was already deeply tanned and his hair had grown back across the shaven scalp and the holes that had been drilled into his head to relieve the pressure when he had collapsed six months previously. His second aneurysm. The doctors had warned him that if he wanted to survive his 96 year old mother he would have to rethink the way he lived.

He considered that he had made quite a few concessions to a long life. He had persuaded his office to pension him off at the age of 60 because of his health problems, cut down on his cigarettes and changed his

1

drinking habits. He had now stocked the boat with a large quantity of fine brandy and his favourite Brunello di Montalcino red. He had given up the cheap stuff forever. As far as Leonardo was concerned, a ship's ballast should always be drinkable.

He stretched out in the cockpit and listened to the pleasant rhythm of the stays banging against the mast. On the far shore of the Fiumara River someone was using an electric sander on their boat's hull. On this bank, used for boats that did not need any heavy work done to them, he was alone, which was the way he liked it. He decided not to drive back to Rome that evening. He much preferred being on *Elisir* than in his gloomy apartment in the Monteverde district, still reverberating with echoes of his mother's false piety and his own choked-off rage. He wanted to quietly mull over an extremely pleasant day spent celebrating with close friends. Several bottles in his collection had been consumed over a leisurely lunch before he waved them off across the river on the hourly ferry. Now he was finishing off his brandy in blissful solitude. Maybe it was wrong to celebrate the death of his mother, who had looked as if she would outlive everyone she knew. But she had been a tyrant who had made his life hell and sent his father to an early grave, and all he felt was relief.

While opening their third bottle of wine he had told his friends that, for the first time since he could remember, he felt optimistic about the future. This declaration had been met with much laughter, given his usual cynical outlook on life, but once they had pulled themselves together and sat up again, or as close to upright as they could get at that stage, they had offered him encouragement, and he was still basking in the unusual sensation of being almost happy. A sudden loud thud against the hull, and his eyes snapped open. He must have nodded off for a while. He got up to investigate the noise: probably a log drifting down to the sea. They usually just scraped along the side and then got caught in the current again. Gripping the metal rigging with one hand, Leonardo peered over at the sluggish brown water. Sure enough, there was a log sidling along towards his distorted reflection. He had no illusions about his appearance: he looked his age and then some. From this distance, though, with his thick hair, slight build and rare smile of contentment, he looked a bit like the boy he had once been, before he got old and grumpy. The log slid through his reflection and at the same moment pain seized his head, vice-like, and squeezed. He only had time to remember not taking his medicine the previous night, time to swear at the Madonna and all the saints, and even to grin ruefully at having to die just when he had decided that life was worth living, before he fell.

The cold water shocked a little sense back into him but his reactions were far too slow. He was not sure where the surface was, floundering in his waterlogged clothes, holding on to the breath he had in his lungs, because it would surely be his last.

So this is it. Why fight against it anyway? Life has mostly been pretty damn miserable so why should the future be any better? His cynicism, as usual, got the upper hand and mocked him. *That is what you get for feeling hopeful, thinking you could start again.* Oh, the irony of drowning, for *him,* who avoided swimming from his beloved *Elisir* at all times, staying dry like a sun-loving cat all summer, clutching a gin-and-tonic and watching his friends splash around the boat as she bobbed at anchor in many a crystalline bay. Now, when he drowned, it was going to be in this stinking, putrid river. It was not the dignified end he would have wished for.

You always read about people dying who see their whole lives rolling out before them. Leonardo, waiting for the dull movie to begin, was surprised when all that happened was an overwhelming conviction that his whole life had been building up to this moment. All his sad and dreary days, his depression and negativity had steered him inexorably to this point, and for some reason he found that immensely funny — and if he had not been in this predicament he would have laughed.

Instead, he held on to his remaining air stubbornly, but he knew that soon the pressure would build up too much and he would have to take that last instinctive gasp for fresh air. *Dying is easy*, he realised, *all I have to do is let go.* Then, just as on every normal day of his life, his thoughts triggered a song in his mind and Annie Lennox sang the sweet refrain, like a soundtrack to his life:

'*Dying is easy, it's living that scares me to death ....*' How absurd, he thought. Even my dying is accompanied by a song in my head, only this time I will not have to be bothered by it continually butting into my thoughts for the rest of the day. Pondering the farcical nature of life, which seemed to be continuing right up to the point of death, he let the rest of the air in his lungs slide out of his mouth.

The bubbles appeared strangely beautiful as they trickled away, and suddenly he had an intelligent thought. If the bubbles were moving, the direction in which they were going had to be up. With enormous effort he forced his body to turn, and kicked his feet feebly to follow the bubbles. Vague sunlight filtered through the muddy water and now the memory of sun on his shoulders and the play of light on rippling water ignited some small spark of hope in his mind. He kicked again, and — if this *had* been a film of his life — right now the soundtrack would be blaring out the music from *Rocky* as Balboa runs triumphantly up the steps of the Philadelphia Museum of Art. With the upward surge, hope raced around Leonardo's body and then his head bashed into something hard.

Bugger it, I am under the boat, was his first thought, *Marconi's luck right to the very end!* Then the pressure above him eased and his head broke free of the water, nose grating along the damn log that had caused him to fall overboard in the first place. Leonardo grabbed at the log which dipped and bobbed sidewise as if asking him to dance. *Sainted mother of Christ,* he hissed, spitting out filthy water and dragging blissful air into his lungs, then reached feebly for the log again. This time he managed to grasp it. *Maybe there really is a God, let's hope he doesn't decide to punish me now for all the imprecations I have just hurled at him,* Leonardo scolded himself, realising that by grabbing at the log he had changed its trajectory and sent it sideways between *Elisir* and the next boat along. Wedged between the boats, forked end stuck fast in the water reeds growing under the jetty, the log made a rough and slimy pillow for his head.

Leonardo realised that he was raving. The pain in his head was overwhelming, his sight blurred. His smoke-damaged lungs were raw from the foul water and he had so little strength left that he was not sure how long he would be able to hold onto the slippery wood. Another thought struck him. The only possibility of his being saved now was the ferryman — and the last ferry came across to this shore at 6pm. He did not have the strength to lift his arm and see if his watch was still working, but suddenly a weight lifted from Leonard's heart and this life, on which he had such a tenuous hold, seemed funny, bright and impossibly beautiful. He wanted more of it. He wanted to do all the things that he never had, wanted travel, love, laughter. Part of him had died in that river. The part that was left was going to hold on to life with every particle of strength left in him.

It was Leonardo's hysterical laughter that saved his life. The ferryman heard it as he tied up, and — alarmed by the manic sound of it — walked along the jetty and found Leonardo clinging to the log. The ferryman swore to his wife that night that the half-drowned man had surely lost his mind. It was enough to give him the creeps whenever he thought of it. As he'd grabbed Mr Marconi by his shirt collar and dragged him onto the jetty, the poor man was babbling about someone else in the river, someone called Leo who had drowned. As he hauled him along the jetty to the ferry, Mr Marconi had kept laughing, weakly waving one arm and shouting goodbye and good riddance to someone who was not there, except in his mind.

2

A Troublesome Client

Miss Angelina Snow shook her hips, fascinated by the huge ruby in her tummy button that glinted in the sultry light of the candlelit tent. Her wrist and ankle bracelets jangled merrily in time with the rhythm of the music in her head, as the singer sang about crossing the desert to reach her with a smile. Then, as the chorus of *'Take me I'm Yours'* penetrated her consciousness, she opened her eyes. She was smiling broadly as she swung her legs out of bed. Dreams were such fun, especially when they involved flowing kaftans and a dark-skinned sheikh wearing hardly any clothes.

Outside her flat the rain was beating down. A typical English summer's day. She twitched the curtains aside, and as the droplets raced each other down the window pane, she frowned as she tried to work out who the sheikh reminded her of. His face had seemed oddly familiar, although she was sure she knew nobody like that. But then dreams were often like that.

She pushed her large, rather bony feet into a pair of well-worn men's leather slippers and went into the bathroom. Then a quick shower, water pattering merrily on the shower cap she always pulled over her sleek grey bob to keep it exactly that way. '*Take me I'm yours, because dreams are made of this,*' she sang loudly, still smiling at the memory of her dream. Briskly, she rubbed herself with a towel. A squidge of moisturiser rubbed into her skin, hair shaken free and brushed to a sheen, and teeth attacked vigorously — and she was almost transformed into her business-like self again. As she flapped back into her bedroom, however, she noticed that she was still humming the tune from her dream. Her lips twitched — thank goodness her mind had not gone on to play another track from the album she had been listening to the previous night, on a rare nostalgia trip. Who knows what dream it would have conjured up to accompany '*A Little Slap and Tickle*'?

She opened her wardrobe and selected her clothes quickly, making a mental note to avoid listening to music with lyrics before going to bed. A little gentle Chopin or sultry saxophone would not stimulate her imagination so much. She chose a severe navy trouser suit and exchanged her tatty slippers for black leather ankle boots with a two inch heel. Tucking the slippers back under her bed, as always, made her remember her Dad. Her first pair of slippers like these had been his. She had taken them from his bedside after he had died and worn them every day after that, until they had fallen to pieces. Then she had bought herself an identical pair because they helped her to remember the loving, gentle man she missed continually.

At the door she took a long khaki raincoat from the coat hook and slipped it over her impeccable tailoring, adding a wide-brimmed slouch hat and umbrella as a precaution against the rain which was still hurling itself at her windows. The streets of Bourne were empty at 8.30am. Her high heels clicked beautifully on the wet pavement. She was a woman who liked to make a noise when she walked, especially in places where silence was expected. It was very therapeutic to know you had the ability to irritate people just by striding along with your head up.

Greeting the few acquaintances she passed, Angelina was aware of a certain reserve which she did nothing to change, keeping her nod cool and never slowing her pace. Taller than most people anyway, with her heels she was an impressive sight. In fact, whilst in her youth Angelina had been described as 'striking' by those few courageous men to have courted her, nowadays the adjective most frequently used about her was 'formidable'.

A. Snow, Estate Agent was only a short walk from her flat. She jangled the office keys in her deep coat pocket and revised her day's appointments. First of the day was Mr Marconi. She frowned at the thought of her most troublesome client and then suddenly realised that the sheikh in her dream had reminded her of him for some inexplicable reason, even though the contrast between them could not have been greater. While both were olive-skinned and hawk-nosed, the sheikh had been resplendent in billowing white silk trousers and bare brown chest. The real Mr Marconi had a preference for quality sweaters, neatly-pressed jeans and expensive boat shoes, and was slightly pigeon-chested. He also had a remarkable mastery of English for an Italian, with quite a plummy accent and a dry sense of humour. Most of these were traits that she appreciated, but — she stopped in her tracks and scowled, making a passer-by swerve to avoid her. Angelina shook her head in exasperation. What on earth was she thinking of? She was not in the habit of awarding points to men for eligibility and even if she had, Mr Marconi would certainly not have been top of the list. In reality, he remained her most irritating client. So far, she had shown him nearly every house she had on her books for rent, and he had found fault with them all.

Folding her umbrella, she pushed open the door to *The Bean Bag* and ordered coffee and a toasted teacake to take away. As she left, the lady behind her greeted the waitress with a friendly, 'Morning, me duck.'

No one ever had the temerity to call Angelina 'me duck' but as she stepped back into the driving rain she thought the local greeting was particularly apt today. The office was only five doors away, so she left her umbrella closed and dashed through the torrent, hoping the teacake would not get wet. Wrestling with keys, coffee and umbrella she got the office door open and thankfully slammed it behind her. Five minutes later she was sitting behind her desk, looking her usual sleek and elegant self. The teacake was gone and the coffee half finished, her diary and papers had been consulted and straightened. Now she braced herself for the arrival of her trainee, Julie.

There were times when Angelina regretted having such a soft heart. If she were made of sterner stuff, she would have said no to the girl at her interview, but she had a weakness for a sweet smile and pleading eyes — and apart from the fact that Julie could not understand the concept of speaking quietly, she was actually very efficient and so she stayed.

Just as Angelina was wondering where she had got to this morning, Julie rushed by the window and flung open the door. What a peculiar raincoat — transparent, with a hood on which perched a mini multi-coloured umbrella. Seen through the raincoat were what they had compromised on as being correct office wear. At Julie's interview Angelina had specified a suit, either with a skirt or with trousers. She had neglected to be specific about colour. Today's suit was a boxy little number in red and pink with white sandals to complete the look.

'Hiya, Miss Snow. It's really pissing down out there.' Julie said, beaming at her boss as she shook her raincoat over the office carpet, then flipped her long blonde plait out of her jacket and settled herself at the reception desk. As she ran her finger down the appointment page, commenting irreverently about the clients as she did so, Angelina noticed with fascination that Julie's nails seemed to be painted with miniature Union Jack flags today. Something to do with a football game, she discovered after Julie saw her staring at them.

'Great, aren't they? My mate Trisha done them for me last night.'

'This would be Trisha of the purple streaks?'

'Yeah. Fancy doing *that* to your hair! Mind you, her real colour is just boring old mousey brown, so I suppose she had to do *something* to it, what with working in an 'airdresser's an all.' Julie smoothed her plait, of which she was justifiably proud, and went back to scrutinising the diary.

'Oh' she squeaked, turning quite pink, 'you didn't tell me your brother was coming today.'

'He rang after you left last night.'

Angelina smiled indulgently, herself thrilled by the prospect of seeing Hal. Julie had a bit of a crush on him. He had that effect on women of all ages, with his warm, blue-eyed smile and easy banter. At thirty-five, he still possessed a boyish optimism which charmed everyone he met. In fact, he was her opposite in just about every way, it seemed to Angelina. They were physically very similar, but the same features that made Hal so attractive; being tall and thin with a strong jaw and Roman nose, did not flatter his sister. Angelina adored Hal. He was more like a son than a brother to her, though. He was seventeen years younger than her, the child of their father's second marriage, and she had brought him up from the age of three, when their father and his second wife had been killed in a car crash.

Glancing at her watch, Angelina saw that she had ten minutes before her appointment with Mr Marconi. Settling back in her leather chair, she faked interest in her computer screen to avoid more conversation and happily began to plan where to take Hal that evening.

Twenty minutes later Angelina was fuming. The rain was slowing somewhat, but Mr Marconi was late — a good ten minutes late. Knowing that Hal was coming had put Julie into a garrulous mood that no amount of ignoring, snapping and huffing could quell. Angelina tapped at her computer keyboard and refused to be drawn into conversation, but her ears betrayed her and listened anyway.

'So, I was calling him Mr Marconi and he said, ever so polite-like, that I could call him *Layo* and I said *Lee-oh* and he said no, Italians pronounce it *Layo*. So, I said I couldn't do that 'cause Miss Snow would kill me and he said to make it more formal and call him *Lay-o-nah-do*. That made me giggle. Well, it sounds funny, doesn't it? He smiled too and he is really nice when he smiles. His face goes all kind of crinkly, all over.'

'Enough! Julie, I cannot concentrate with you chattering on. Where is the blasted man, anyway? Punctuality was the only thing I had come to expect from him, apart from the inevitability of his disliking every property I have taken him to.'

Julie's 'Oooh-oh, *who*'s in a bad mood then?' went unchecked, because right then Mr Marconi was seen getting out of the passenger seat of a car which had double-parked outside the office and was blocking the traffic in the high street. The driver waved at Mr Marconi and then waved to Miss Snow and Julie in the office too before driving off.

'You can tell they're Italians by the way they drive. He's really good looking, that Marco from the restaurant, isn't he?'

'*Julie,*' Angelina growled; and this time the girl took notice and got ready to greet Mr Marconi with her brightest smile.

'Morning,' said Julie breezily as Mr Marconi pushed open the door. He nodded at Julie while brushing away the few raindrops that had dared to land on his dark-grey rain-jacket. It pained her to admit it, but Julie was right — Mr Marconi's crinkly smile *was* nice. It was also rare, and as soon as he turned to her it had been replaced by his habitual sardonic look. Angelina stood up swiftly, heading off further chitchat as she yanked on her raincoat and hat and reached for her umbrella.

'Shall we go, Mr Marconi?' she asked.

Holding the door open for him, she noted with pleasure the quality of his jacket.

'See ya, Miss Snow. Bye — Layonahdo!' Julie screeched — and Angelina winced. She would have to have another word with the girl about the appropriate decibel level for office use. As Julie swung her plait and crossed her legs, Angelina noticed Mr Marconi's appreciative gaze. Julie did not seem at all unaware of the effect she was having, the little minx! Another thing to bring to her attention at a later date.

'She *is* very young,' she said curtly as they stepped outside. Marconi looked at her solemnly.

'Have you met her mother?' he asked.

'Yes — so...?'

'And is she older and wiser?'

'Oh dear.' Angelina considered Mrs Clark for a moment and felt a sudden rush of affection for Julie.

The rain had started up again and Mr Marconi was looking at it dubiously, so to avoid further delays she started walking and waited for him to catch her up.

'The house is in a new development and is within easy walking distance.' She opened the umbrella with a flourish as she began her sales spiel.

'Did you say that it was within *walking* distance or marching distance?' Marconi asked innocently, and she waited until her spontaneous grin had faded before slowly turning towards him. The man immediately took advantage of her pause to duck into a doorway and shake himself like a wet dog. Rain pounded on her umbrella and her feet felt damp already, but it would just not be British to give in to the elements.

'Mr Marconi, surely you must have rain in Italy,' she coaxed, fighting the urge to laugh.

'Yes, dear lady, of course and when we do we usually wait in a shop doorway, or preferably a bar, until it has passed.' As he spoke, Marconi gestured to window of the shop he was sheltering by. A red *Sale* notice hung on the door and the window was crammed with ladies' clothes and underwear that ranged from flirty lace to huge, substantial beige items that defied the imagination.

'Well, unless you find the underwear sale more interesting than I do, we had better move or risk staying here for a week, and delightful as I find your company ….'

Marconi surprised her by laughing. Then, (the utter *cheek* of the man), he stepped under her umbrella next to her and took hold of the handle just above her hand so that their fingers touched.

Angelina was used to towering over other people and used her height to great advantage, making sure to wear high heels as well. She believed that plain women had a duty to make a statement and use whatever resources they had in order to compensate for their lack of prettiness.

She had found that a lot of women and most men were intimidated by her, but not so Mr Marconi. He seemed completely at ease walking alongside her. He did not seem bothered by her height or his own lack of it. From her elevated viewpoint she could admire his thick black hair, heavily streaked with grey. He was urbane and spoke English almost like a native. Indeed, it was his voice that caught one's attention, beautifully modulated and deep, with a hint of suppressed humour. If she were the kind of woman who believed in romance, she might be tempted to get to know him better. But of course, she was not, and so put the thought aside firmly.

'Shall we jump in puddles too?' he inquired. Angelina managed to ignore him magnificently, even his continuous humming of the very inappropriate *O Sole Mio* until they reached the house, where Angelina got her revenge by showering him with rain as she vigorously closed the umbrella and leant it against the frame of the porch.

As Angelina ushered Mr Marconi inside, she had to admit that the new estate did not look its best in the rain. The gardens had not been established long enough to give any colour, and the road was muddy from the workmen's trucks. This side of the estate had been finished but they were still working on the other. This being a new house, there was a vague possibility that Mr Marconi might like it, since he would not be able to complain that there was an odd smell or that the windows let in draughts. She prided herself on being able to match her clients with the right home but Mr Marconi had her confused. It was also intriguing trying to find out what made him tick. She watched him attentively as he stood in the middle of the small front room and caught herself beginning to hum out loud too. '*Take me, I'm yours,*' — *that* tune again. She hoped he had not recognised the song. It was doubtful that an Italian would know music from her teenage days, but with Mr Marconi she had learnt not to make such assumptions. He beamed at her.

'The trouble with catchy songs is that they sneak up on you and you find yourself humming them all day, even at the most inopportune moments,' he said sympathetically. 'Great group, Squeeze. I used to really like them,' he added, and she felt her cheeks growing hot.

'There is a lot of light in here,' she said hopefully, changing the subject, and was pleased to see him nod. He looked at the staircase that ran up from the lounge.

'Two nice-size bedrooms. One for guests — or you could use it as a study.' Yes, that was right, he liked the idea of a study. He had told her that he was retired, over here visiting his cousin; that he had already had enough of living with his family and needed his own space, and that Bourne seemed as good a place as any for him to live for a year or so. To *rest my mind and recover my life* had been the intriguing way he had phrased it. Feeling a bit more confident, Angelina told him that the house had never been lived in and had been a show house.

'Ah, that explains the lime green. Why do designers do that?' he wondered. 'Even with a bit of brown leather it still makes me feel nauseous.'

Angelina was not ready to give up and whisked him through the nice open-plan archway into the dining/kitchen space, bravely declaring the modern fitted kitchen to be the house's best feature. Marconi shook his head.

'My dear, it has a *breakfast bar*!'

Now Angelina was truly bemused. What possible fault could a single man find with a breakfast bar? His eyes twinkled as he pulled out a stylish chrome and leather bar-stool and gestured towards it.

'Unfortunately for me, I do not have your wonderfully long legs. By the time I had managed to haul myself up Everest to perch my bottom on this stool, I would have lost interest in my toast and coffee. Imagine the horror of settling myself in front of a plate of *Spaghetti all' Amatriciana*, with a wonderful bottle of *Brunello* and then realising that I had forgotten the corkscrew and would have to renegotiate the perils of the perch to get it!'

Angelina sighed. She wanted to laugh but had an idea that he was actually serious about dining in comfort.

'OK, Mr Marconi. I will add that to my long, *long* list of things to avoid. No breakfast bars!'

3

Dining with the Drowned

The restaurant was crowded but Marco had kept a small table free for his uncle in the corner by the kitchen, and Leonardo was half-way through his *antipasto* of prosciutto and melon, and considerably more than half-way through a bottle of Brunello di Montalcino. He sat with his back to the kitchen so that he had a view of the other diners, in particular the table by the door where his frosty estate agent, Miss Snow, was sitting with a man who was a lot younger than her. She did not look at all icy tonight, though. She was laughing and gesticulating in the manner of a woman having a very good time. Leonardo stuck his fork hard into a recalcitrant square of melon and succeeded in shooting it off the plate and under the feet of a passing waitress. She jumped nimbly to one side without losing her grip on the pile of plates she was taking back to the kitchen, and his eagle-eyed nephew fixed him with a frown as he moved to welcome a couple who had just come in.

Not only was Miss Snow making a fool of herself with a toy-boy, she was wearing something completely unexpected. Instead of wearing her usual business-like and impeccably tailored suit, she was revealing enough chest for everyone to see that she had nothing to hide, in a low-cut, silky dress that barely covered her knees. Her legs went on and on, covered in shiny pale stockings and finally ended up in a pair of elegant court shoes with a tapering heel. Leonardo raised his glass morosely and took a long drink. He contemplated the black-and-chrome, subtly-lit and stylish interior of *Il Toscano* with a frown.

When he had been released from the hospital after his brush with death in the filthy Tevere River he had wanted to get as far away from his old life as possible. In the end he had decided to make the visit to his cousin Luigi (his one remaining relative) that he had been promising for years. Luigi had moved to Bourne as a young man, and opened the family-run Italian restaurant, which was doing very well. Leonardo had been welcomed into the family without hesitation and settled into the small annex that Luigi and Anna had converted for their son Carlo when he had been a bachelor. Carlo was now married, with three small children. Leonardo's other nephew, Marco, had kindly moved out of the annex he had inherited and was back in his childhood bedroom. Leonardo felt a bit guilty about that but had not intended to stay long. Although he enjoyed the fuss that they had made of him it was hard to think with the noise of an extended family around him all the time. However, he had not had any idea where to go from there, until, one day, while walking through the town, he had looked into the window of *A. Snow, Estate Agent* and found a reason to stay. It was Miss Snow's height that had first attracted him. She had been adding property details to the window so that he could only see the parts of her that showed in between the cards: grey hair swinging around one ear, the point of her chin, long, slim fingers with well-manicured nails but no rings and those legs, from her knees to just above her ankles. That day she had been wearing a slim-fitting black suit with a skirt that ended above the knees, and black stiletto-heeled shoes, which he had appreciated very much on entering the office. Her strong face with its rather haughty expression and cool, grey eyes could never be described as beautiful or even particularly feminine, and her brusque manner was not alluring, but it was certainly challenging — and so Leonardo had embarked on his house-seeking mission.

He had thoroughly enjoyed being shown around the different houses for rent that Miss Snow took him to, but he had absolutely no intention of taking any of them until he had worn down her defences. He had felt a definite thawing towards him today. She had even had to suppress a smile at a few of his quips and he was beginning to feel that the time had come to ask her out for dinner. Now — there she was, flirting with some young, blonde, muscular kid. What could she *possibly* see in him? Marco came and removed his antipasto plate.

'Everything OK, *Zio*?' he asked, raising an eyebrow in a way that managed to look both amused and concerned.

'*Si, si*,' Leonardo answered irritably, and poured himself another glass of wine. It was then that he noticed that the other chair at his little table for two, which had previously been empty, was now occupied by a hazy shape that he knew he should recognise from somewhere.

'*Have another drink and forget about women. You have never had any luck with them so why should you think anything has changed? Stick to the wine — that won't let you down,*' the shape urged wisely, and Leonardo nodded in agreement. The waitress brought his *Saltimbocca alla Romana*, momentarily blocking his view, and he sniffed appreciatively. When he glanced back at his companion he had a moment of utter shock and disbelief. His hazy friend was *himself*; a ghostly impression of *himself* complete with drink in hand, cynical expression and very wet clothes. He immediately looked at the wine bottle and swiftly calculated how many glasses he had drunk. Enough to feel pleasantly warmed but certainly not enough to cause him to hallucinate. Drowned Leo raised his glass and Leonardo mirrored the gesture. He experimented a bit with this unprecedented phenomenon, adding a few details to his mental creation. Seconds later Drowned Leo was knocking cigarette ash onto the table cloth and making Leonardo wish he could do the same. Cutting down was hell, and these days smoking in restaurants was just not allowed. His *alter ego* looked around him and shook his head in disapproval.

'*What on earth do you see in her anyway? Those cold grey eyes. She's built like a coat hanger. Imagine cuddling up to that!*' he declared, and drained his wine glass. Leonardo did the same and then refilled it.

'*Mio Dio*,' he exclaimed out loud, and rubbed his eyes. When he opened them again Miss Snow was standing over him, looking at him in a rather puzzled way.

'May I sit down?' she asked. Leonardo was unsure how to answer since, as far as he was aware, the seat was already occupied by a soggy, phantom version of himself, grinning sardonically across the table at him and shaking his head at the impossibility that this new life he had embarked on could ever work out.

Miss Snow made a loud tutting noise of irritation, yanked back the chair, and sank down into it, smoothing the soft grey silk of her skirt over her legs. She had, in one gesture, utterly annihilated any trace of his drowned doppelganger. What a marvellous woman!

'Would you care for a glass?' Leonardo asked the steely-eyed coat hanger.

'No thank you, I have had quite enough already,' she replied, and then added sternly 'and so have you, I believe, Mr Marconi.'

Given that he was conjuring up vivid visions of a drowned man, Leonardo concluded that she was probably quite right.

'My brother and I were wondering if you would like to join us for coffee and dessert, once you have finished your meal.' Miss Snow indicated the rapidly congealing meat in front of him and Leonardo did not hesitate to push his plate away and stand up. All at once he felt much better. His doppelganger had been squashed beneath Miss Snow's behind, and the young man she was dining with was her brother.

'With pleasure, dear lady,' he informed her, and gallantly gave her his hand to help her rise. Before he followed her across the room, Leonardo stared hard at the chair Miss Snow had been sitting in and found it reassuringly empty.

***

It was something of a relief for Angelina to conclude that Mr Marconi was not, after all, even slightly interested in her. For a while that afternoon she had wondered if he was trying to flirt with her and thought she would have to put him in his place, but had finally decided that he was just behaving like any Italian man around a member of the opposite sex. As she ate her dinner she had seen him sitting across the room, looking glum, and had idly mentioned him to Hal as her most irritating client. Hal, typically impulsive and generous, had said, 'Well, why not invite him over to join us for coffee?' Then, as soon as she had introduced them and mentioned in passing that Hal was here only for one night since he hated sleeping on dry land and was always in a rush to get back to his boat, Mr Marconi had not looked at her once. As soon as the fatal word BOAT was spoken, he underwent a most remarkable transformation. The elderly man with his crumpled, sombre face vanished and was replaced by something remarkably ... Italian. His body became animated. His arms, clad in quality, pale lemon cotton, came alive as he gesticulated with enthusiasm. He looked about twenty years younger.

'What kind of boat?' he asked eagerly, and listened raptly to Hal's ecstatic description of *Calypso*. Angelina tuned out. Her view of Hal's home differed vastly from his. Where he saw freedom and adventure she remembered sharp, bruising corners, low ceilings designed to knock out any hapless visitor and an overwhelming odour of engine grease and bilges. She was far more interested in Mr Marconi's transformation. He urged Hal to call him Leo, laughed and joked, and swapped stories with increasing hilarity. The two men became breathless with laughter on the subject of women on board. What a waste of water they caused with their constant, unnecessary *washing*, and what havoc they caused to the bilge pumps by shedding all that *hair*!

Angelina had stayed on *Calypso* only once, just after Hal had bought her. She remembered him being unusually stern as he gave her instructions on how to behave on board, in particular how to comb her hair. Standing at the stern the following morning in the cold April wind while following his instructions to always comb her hair down-wind and on deck, she had vowed never to set foot on board again. She had dutifully dragged the brush through her hair, without a mirror for guidance, then turned to head back into the warmth for her coffee, but by the time she had reached shelter her hair was in a worse state than when she had woken up.

It turned out that Mr Marconi had just sold the beautiful *Elisir*, a 50ft Sciarrelli schooner and absolute paragon of a sailing boat. He regretted it enormously, and now, having discovered that Hal's passion for the sea equalled his own, they were deep in a discussion about the inevitability of osmosis in old vessels and what type of top-coat gave the best finish for perfect woodwork.

Angelina sat back and sipped her coffee, trying not to feel excluded.

'Lili is not as fond of boats as us, Leo, and I think we are probably boring her. Am I right, sis, or am I right? Hal asked, winking at her. Mr Marconi noticed her presence once more and she had to laugh at the expression of disbelief she saw in his eyes when she agreed with Hal.

'Really Mr Marconi, I can honestly say that I find the idea of living on a boat the way Hal does to be a downright uncomfortable experience, even when he is moored up somewhere nice and safe. I have no intention of discovering just how unnerving it would be at sea.'

It was obvious that Mr Marconi was about to wax lyrical about the joys of boat life again but fortunately, before he could, Hal butted in.

'What is all this *Mr Marconi* and *Miss Snow* business?' he asked.

Formality had never been Hal's way, a fact that had caused him numerous problems in his school days. As his guardian she had been constantly called in to discuss his cheeky attitude and lack of application. In fact, the only thing that Hal had really excelled in at school had been getting into trouble; like the time he had stolen the maths teacher's glasses and glued them to the statue of the honourable founder of the school which graced its inner courtyard, or the day that he had argued with a master and been found an hour later sitting on the school roof. He had said that he needed to get away and breathe some fresh air. He had been quite malleable at his local junior school, but once she had sent him away to the public school their father had attended he had become a real rebel. It was only when Angelina had agreed that he could move back home and go to the local comprehensive that he had reverted to his former happy and charming self.

'Come on Lili, lighten up,' Hal urged, and Mr Marconi obviously agreed with him, leaning forward to consider her. His countenance was rearranged into its usual gloomy and slightly mournful lines now that he was no longer thinking about the sea.

'Lili?' he mused. 'I thought you would be an Amanda or Alison because of the letter A on your office window.'

Angelina sighed. Her name was one of the banes of her life and she knew that Hal would not be able to resist telling the story of their father's odd choices. Sure enough, Hal launched into the familiar explanation.

'Lili is my name for her, Leo. Her name is actually Angelina, but when I was young I couldn't say Angelina and used to call her Lili and it just stuck. Dad was inventive with our names. He took one look at his first-born, this remarkably long, dark-haired baby, and decided to call her Angelina.'

'Can you imagine growing up looking like me and being called *little angel snow* or, later on, having the same name as one of the sexiest actresses in Hollywood?' Angelina raised her eyebrows in irritation.

'Too bad, sis, I agree, but then he gave me an equally hard name to live with,' Hal chipped in, laughing, and clearly enjoying himself.

Leonardo was studying her far too attentively for her liking. Angelina was annoyed to feel herself begin to blush.

'I assumed that Hal was an abbreviation of Henry,' he said, finally turning back to Hal.

'Oh no, nothing that simple for Dad,' Hal said, shaking his head. 'My real name is Halliwell, but I have spent all my life denying it. Dad said it was an old English name that meant *holy well*. With our names and surname you can see that Dad was keen on purity.'

Leonardo looked at him intensely and nodded.

'Fathers are like that, giving us names that we have to live up to. My father named me after Da Vinci, but fortunately Leonardo is a very common name in Italy. So is Angelina, you know. I suppose your father must have named you both for what he saw in you, through the eyes of love.'

'How poetic!' Angelina responded sharply, putting an end to the conversation in exasperation. He really did have the nicest voice though, she admitted to herself. So deep and melodic with just an occasional hint of a foreign lilt. He gave her one of his rare smiles, creasing his weather-beaten face up in that crinkly way that Julie had remarked on earlier. Then he turned back to Hal with a question about England's problematic tides, and she sighed.

This looked like it was going to be a very long evening, and yet it had started out so promisingly. For once, Hal had seemed to have other things than sailing on his mind. She suspected that there was a new woman in his life, maybe an important one, and she had genuinely wanted to find out more. However once Mr Marconi had joined them, the conversation had moved onto other subjects and the moment had passed. Perhaps she should have left him sitting there in his corner, after all. That way she would have avoided the endless tales of engine maintenance and the joys of self-tailing winches.

4

Saying Grace

Angelina settled comfortably into the corner of her sofa and gazed at Hal in amusement over the rim of her glass. She was glad to be alone with him in a place where she felt completely at ease. She had found the evening quite challenging. There was something about Mr Marconi that got under her skin, stirring up emotions that she did not want stirred. She could not stop thinking about what he had told them earlier, when Hal had asked what had brought him to Bourne, of all places.

Hal's amazing ability of getting people to open up, drawing even the most closed individuals out of their shells, had worked on crusty old Mr Marconi too. She had seen him sparkle with joy as he and Hal discussed boat life, but had a feeling that he had been quite surprised too, to find himself telling them about his brush with death. She had noticed him hesitate a few times, flicking swift glances in her direction to gauge her reaction, as he related his story in a matter-of-fact way, even making fun of his traumatic experience at times. He told them about his relief at discovering which way the surface of the filthy river lay, only to come up under a log and whack his head, which was already on the point of exploding. Then he had rubbed his head — as if he could still feel the bump — with such a woeful expression that she and Hal had burst out laughing.

At the end of the tale, Hal had said, 'So, you have a second chance to recreate a life that you really want, Leonardo. I understand that you wanted to be looked after by your family for a while, but what on earth is keeping you here now? I think you should head for the Caribbean or—' Before Hal could start on about the superb anchorages he had read about around the world, Angelina had leant across the table and touched Mr Marconi's hand, feeling profoundly moved. Looking him in the eye she had told him that she was very glad that he had survived.

'One awkward client fewer for you if I hadn't,' he had quipped, but she could tell that her words had touched him.

She tore her mind away from Mr Marconi and smiled at Hal. He had taken her beautifully co-ordinated cushions from the sofa and was sprawled across them on the floor. His Armagnac was untouched beside him, and if he was not a bit more careful with his gestures she could see it getting spilt over her precious cushions. His apparel was testimony to his lack of concern as far as stains were concerned. He was wearing his home clothes, as he called them; clothes that he left at her house and changed into as soon as he got through the door. These choice items consisted of an old pair of grey tracksuit bottoms and a T-shirt, where the design of a motorbike was considerably enhanced by what appeared to be oil stains and something yellow, maybe egg. He smelt clean, though. Each time he left after staying with her, Angelina carefully washed and ironed these same clothes, eternally hopeful of getting rid of the marks. Then she would fold them gently and put them away in the airing cupboard to make sure they would always be warm and ready for his visits. Hal made another violent gesture as he described his prowess in a recent regatta and Angelina made an involuntary start of protest toward the brandy.

'Sorry sis, I forgot,' he told her, and took a large sip.

'Did you think I might make a mess? I wouldn't *dare*. This place is as immaculate as you are,' he teased, and chucked a cushion at her. Angelina batted it away easily. Hal had honed her instincts well over the years. She smoothed a hand over her skirt, enjoying the sensuous feel of the silk. It was true, she was an elegant creature and loved to surround herself with beautiful things.

'Immaculate, elegant and so very cool, Miss A Snow. Don't you ever want to let go so people can get to know the real you?' Hal cocked his head on one side, clearly expecting a serious answer.

'Darling Hal, I am as I am. I am exactly this way with everyone because that is my true nature. I have no desire to open up to the world. I enjoy my life just as it is. It is only you who manages to unsettle my beautifully ordered life, you little pest! And you only manage it because you have had a lifetime to practise irritating me.' Now it was her turn to tease. Leaning forward she asked innocently, 'So, are you going to tell me about her or not?' Laughing at her brother's surprise, she shook her head at him.

'Hal, you are quite transparent, you know. You have talked about everything —*except* what really brought you here today, and for that reason I am guessing that it has to be a young lady and that she must be important to you. Am I right?'

Hal nodded. He crossed his legs and hugged his knees to his chest, a gesture she knew so well. From childhood, whenever he needed to tell her something important he would hug his knees. She realised that this time Hal was serious, and hoped fervently that she would like this girl, though she feared she would probably turn out to be just like all the rest. So far Hal had charmed more women than Angelina could count, and she had dried the tears of a few of his exes over the years. He never took life too seriously and was very honest about his need for complete freedom, so that somehow he managed to stay friends with his women after the love affair ended.

Hal did not live by other people's rules. He lived on his old sailing boat, earning money for its upkeep by writing the odd article for sporting magazines or taking seasonal jobs in local boatyards. It was not only sailing that he loved. He was drawn to anything that gave him an adrenalin rush. Over the years she had medicated the cuts and scratches he came home with after climbing up everything he could: the church spire, the roof of his school, whatever tree he felt challenged by. Then, when he grew up and moved away, she had tried not to imagine the exact details of his exploits: parachuting, rock climbing, pot-holing and scuba diving. She would shudder as he told her about them afterwards, and pretend to find it all very exciting instead of terrifying. Hal had little use for money apart from what he spent on *Calypso*. The only new clothes he ever had were whatever she gave him as birthday and Christmas presents. In fact — Angelina made a mental note here — she would have to get him some more socks. There was a large hole in the sole of his left one.

'Her name is Grace.' Having made up his mind, Hal began to talk. Angelina watched him fondly as he told her about how he had met and fallen in love with this woman. That it *was* love was undeniable. Hal had the kind of face that showed his emotions. He found it hard to hide an untruth, which is how she had always found out about the scrapes he got himself into. He believed that she had a kind of sixth sense, but the reality was that his face revealed every thought that passed through his mind.

It seemed that he had met this girl when he had sawn through part of his finger instead of the wood he was using to make a new shelf. He held up the finger to reassure Angelina that it was still intact and head her off before she started to nag him about hospitals and tetanus shots. He had run out of plasters and it had been a Sunday; most shops were shut but he half-remembered seeing a place in a street nearby that had been open when he had popped out for breakfast.

'It was one of those kind of shops that you like, Lili, with a window full of herbs and creams and soaps. So I thought they would probably have a plaster somewhere and went in.'

'Was it still bleeding?' Angelina asked, imagining the scene with the saw all too vividly.

'God, yes, I couldn't stop it. That was why I bothered to go and see if I could find anyone to help. I wrapped it up in a wad of paper, though, so I wasn't dripping over the shop floor or anything, don't worry.' As if I would, Angelina fretted.

'And that is when I saw her,' Hal continued — and his face softened.

'The shop was full of colour. It was divided up into sort of segments radiating out from the cash desk and each bit was a different colour. It's a great place, a bit odd and full of all sorts of mad things like crystals for therapy and incense and stuff. Anyway, there she was, talking on the phone, but she smiled and waved me in. I felt a bit of a fool standing there with all that girly stuff and I would have left, but then she put down the phone and asked if she could help me. I said probably not, I was just looking for a plaster and I waved my hand at her. Then the next thing I knew she was holding my hand and taking me through to her room in the back. She does all kinds of things like colour therapy and aura massage and whatever back there and that was why she was open that day because she had a client booked and had decided she might as well use the day to do an inventory as well. Anyway, she cleaned me up, rubbed in some kind of stinky ointment and wrapped my finger in a bandage, and wouldn't take any money for her help.'

Hal paused here, clearly uncertain about how much to say. He cleared his throat and then rushed on, 'Lili, I just knew. From the moment she took my hand I knew that she was the one for me.' Encouraged by Angelina's silence, Hal continued, 'I asked her if she was free for dinner and she said yes, so I picked her up when she finished work. Then I walked her back to the boat and cooked dinner.'

'Hal!' Angelina was exasperated. 'Why didn't you take her out to a restaurant?'

'I didn't want to share her with anyone. I managed to find some candles too and made it look pretty. I thought she would like that because of all that stuff in her shop.'

As Hal continued his story, it was clear that he had been attracted to someone as out of sync with society as himself, and with the force of character to capture him. He drained his brandy glass and got up. Leaving the glass on the coffee table, he went to the arm chair where he had tossed his clothes earlier, and picked up his jeans. After rummaging in his back pocket he handed her the rather tattered photo that he had unearthed and sank back to the floor, this time leaning against the sofa with his head resting next to Angelina's knees. While Angelina looked at the snapshot of a pretty, dark-skinned girl with close-cropped hair, Hal spoke in a soft voice at odds with his usual forthright and energetic tone.

Angelina leant forward so as not to miss his words, studying the photo as she listened. Grace had a lovely face, with something peaceful about her eyes.

'Wherever I go, I find Grace,' Hal murmured, 'Sometimes, when I am sailing, it is as if *Calypso* is singing her name. The mainsail flutters and snaps *Grace*, the waves tickle her sides and chuckle *Grace*, the wind sighs *Grace* through the rigging. My whole world reverberates to the sound of her name.'

Suddenly embarrassed, Hal shook his head and said mockingly, 'Good Lord, I sound like a blooming poet – must be the brandy.'

Angelina put out her hand to ruffle her brother's hair. Then she kissed the top of his head gently.

'So, what now?'

'Well, I'm going to ask her to move in with me when I get back. I might give her my Mum's engagement ring — you have it somewhere, don't you?'

Angelina suddenly felt a lot less indulgent toward her brother. She knew people lived together nowadays in the most casual ways, but either Hal was serious about this girl or he wasn't. An engagement ring should *mean* something and she felt reluctant to give Hal his mother's ring — which she had in safe keeping along with her own mother's jewellery — until he was finally ready to grow up. Although Hal was clearly crazy about this Grace, still she saw no signs of real commitment in his demeanour.

'You expect her to move in with you *on the boat*!' Angelina snapped.

'Well, she likes the boat too …' Hal moved away slightly as he tried to gauge her mood.

'I have never met this girl, did not even know you were seeing someone in a serious way and suddenly you are going to ask her to move in with you, but you are not going to ask her to marry you, is that right?' Angelina was aware that she seemed to be contradicting herself, but she genuinely did not know which of these things she was most angry about and they all came tumbling out together.

'Marry! Heavens Lili, *no.* I mean, Grace is wonderful and I am really serious about her, but I am not the marrying type, am I?'

'Are you *ever* going to grow up, Hal? You cannot give someone your mother's engagement ring without her expecting a proposal of marriage. You always rush into things without thinking them through —'

'You do enough thinking for both of us,' Hal retorted crossly.

'What is that supposed to mean?' Angelina hissed and stood up.

'What kind of life do you live, sis? What gives you the right to preach at me about my relationships? You are so cold you would freeze any man who tried to get close to you.'

Hal pushed himself up from the floor and faced his sister, ignoring her icy expression, which would have made most people quake in their shoes. He regretted his words as soon as they had left his mouth, but he was not going to back down yet.

They glared at each other in silence and then Angelina spun on her heels and with a swish of silk, retreated to her bedroom.

5

Snow's Grail

Grace took her time to wrap up the hand-painted silk scarf that her well-dressed customer had chosen as a gift for her granddaughter. She added a small tablet of rose-scented soap — so that the first thing the girl would notice on opening the gift was how good it smelt — then layered pink and purple tissue paper around it and finished the package off with a raffia bow and a small posy of dried lavender.

'How pretty that looks. Thank you, dear.' The lady's pleasure was obvious as she took her purchase, now in a small paper bag with the shop logo on it. Grace beamed with pleasure at having helped an indecisive person choose a gift for someone special, and escorted her to the door with a cheerful 'I hope she likes it.' Actually the lady was so sweetly grateful that Grace wanted to give her a great big hug, but on second thoughts decided it might be a bit over-familiar.

Once the door was closed and she was alone again, Grace went to stand in the centre of the yellow sun painted on the floor, the spokes radiating from it in different colours, repeating in various hues in the walls and displays. The shop smelt fresh, perfumed by bunches of dried herbs, soaps and medicinal teas. Sunlight glinted on the shiny surfaces of burnished metal ornaments and crystals, while scarves, towels and linens added texture in rainbow colours. Grace loved this space. Each customer was special to her and finding the right thing for them was a challenge she enjoyed. Behind her was a desk and armchair where she could be comfortable when the shop was empty, and through a door were her treatment rooms and small kitchen. She usually closed the shop at 1 pm on Wednesdays, when her therapy patients would arrive for their appointments, in reflexology, crystal therapy and reiki. She tried not to see more than three clients on these afternoons so that she could focus on each one properly. Today was Friday, though, so she intended to close the shop early and surprise Hal. Just the thought of Hal was enough to make her light up from within. She felt her 'Hal' smile tugging up the corners of her mouth. Ever since the day that he had first come into her shop, she had been unable to control that smile or suppress the moments of pure joy that rushed through her at unexpected times during the day.

As she made her way towards the kitchen, where she kept her coat and bag, she felt the pressure of a headache that had bothered her all afternoon growing stronger now that she was alone. She stopped for a moment and massaged her temples, trying to rid herself of the uncomfortable feeling of foreboding that was nagging at her. She was just too happy to let unwelcome thoughts intrude for long, though. She glanced at the poem *Snow Grail* she had printed carefully on a chalk board behind her desk. She had found the words *Grail — ephemeral, enticing and tangible as the exquisite kiss of snow,* written by an anonymous poet, in a book about Arthurian legends, and felt a deep connection with them, so she had made a sign out of it and hung the poem on the wall. Until meeting Hal she had not known why the words had been important, but Grace always followed her instincts. She laughed out loud now at the memory of Hal standing in front of her, his hand wrapped in bloody kitchen paper, wondering if she might have a plaster when he so obviously needed a proper dressing.

Grace had long been used to her ability to see auras around people, or a special light that emanated from them or from places. It was something she had inherited from her grandmother and had always seemed very natural to her, saving her more than once from making the wrong kind of friendships or relationships. Her Grandma had taught her to pay attention to her instincts, and they rarely let her down.

This rather gorgeous man in front of her, with his blonde hair flopping over one eye and the smell of sawdust on his clothes, had such a bright and open aura that she had been immediately attracted to him. She had taken his hand in hers and led him to the kitchen, where she had washed his deep cut and bandaged it, aware all the time of an unusual warmth flowing between them. On his way out while he was trying to insist on paying her, and she had laughingly refused, he had looked at the poem and stopped short. He had read it out loud, then turned to her with an irresistible beaming smile, and informed her that if she would not let him pay for her ministrations then she would be forced to allow him to make it up to her in another way and let him take her to dinner.

She had agreed at once.

That evening had been both surprisingly comfortable and astonishingly intense. Instead of taking her to a restaurant, he had picked her up and walked her to his boat, where he had prepared a surprisingly competent dinner for her. She would not have cared if he had served her cardboard instead of steak and sauté potatoes. There was something so bright and shiny about Hal, as if he had been newly minted especially for her. Watching him moving around the small galley with ease, telling her about the special features of this boat he adored, the fridge that opened from the top to help prevent spillages in a gale, and the oven that was fixed so that it could level itself with the rhythm of the waves, Grace had felt her world moving and reforming, a sensation that was centred in her heart and not in the unusual bobbing motion of Hal's home. The capacious fridge had held a bottle of champagne, chilled to perfection, and Hal had clinked glasses with her and then offered her a large bowl of salt and vinegar crisps. She had nibbled her way through a handful of crisps while he devoured the rest with one hand and stirred potatoes with the other. When he had finished cooking the steak and slid it onto a plate where it oozed blood just the way it should, she had informed him as gently as she could that she was a vegetarian. Assuming that they were going to a restaurant, it had not occurred to her to mention this earlier. Instead of being upset, Hal had found it hilarious and rummaged around once more in the fridge for a piece of cheese for her, promising to do better next time.

Hal told her later that evening that when he had read the poem in her shop it had seemed directed at him. After all, it was his surname up there on her wall. He had decided then and there to prove to her just how tangible the kiss of Snow could be. That had happened before the dessert, a giant bar of dark chocolate. Hal was not one to take life slowly, she had been glad to discover.

She had several small blackboards in the shop and at home on which she wrote things that pleased her. Once she found a new word or phrase she would erase the old and write in the new. Looking at the words would make her smile again each time she read them. At the moment she could see the words robin, rainbow and a small list of essential oils she needed to reorder, as well as the poem. She had bought a fish-shaped board for Hal too, and he had hung it in the boat's galley even though he had proclaimed it to be kitsch and daft. It had been left blank for ages and she had teased him, saying that without a word it could not trigger any memories or make him smile. The next time he had made dinner for her she had seen that he had written the word *Grace* on it. The word had never been erased or over-written.

Smiling serenely to herself, Grace shrugged on her coat, slung her bag over her shoulder and picked up her keys. She was going to stop at the shops to buy food for tonight before going to the harbour. It was her turn to cook and she was going to make the spicy pasta sauce that Hal loved. He did not usually eat as much meat as their first date would have implied, and Grace had found out that as long as there was a lot of whatever she made, Hal was happy.

Outside, the wind hit her, tugging at her clothes. She turned her face toward it, uplifted by the elemental power that filled her. As she reached the road that flanked the estuary she looked left towards the pier. Beyond it the sea was white-crested under a glowering sky. Grace was endlessly fascinated by the seascapes the North Yorkshire coast offered.

Her Grandma Clair longed for golden days and the Caribbean heat of her youth that warmed your bones, but Grace loved the wild changeability of northern English weather. The only exception was when Hal was out sailing and a storm began to brew. Then Grace would watch the entrance to the port anxiously until she saw *Calypso* appear.

After buying a jar of tomato sauce, some goat's cheese, bread and a bottle of wine, Grace checked her watch. Hal had said he would be back from his sister's by about seven, so she would have time to visit Grandma Clair, as well as tidying herself up, if she hurried.

***

Grace adored her grandmother, a feisty lady who had never lost the soft Caribbean cadences of her youth and had filled Grace's head with wonderful tales of Jamaica when she was growing up. Thinking of her grandmother's forceful character made her mind turn to Hal's sister. Angelina sounded just as formidable, and Grace wondered if Hal had told Angelina about her. She suspected that this had probably been his real reason for going to Lincolnshire, although he was trying to be very casual and had just said he ought to go for a quick visit. Angelina had brought him up when his parents had died and was very important to him. How would she react to the news that Hal was serious about someone? Oh well, she would find out soon enough. .

6

Rings and Windypits

Hal heard his sister creeping around in her bedroom, trying not to wake him. He nestled further into the quilt, turning to face the back of the sofa to ease his cramped legs. Angelina had a large sofa but it was not long enough or wide enough to house the whole of him, so he tried to rest different body parts at different times, and consequently never slept well when he stayed there. He would not move, though, until Angelina had left. He would pretend to be asleep so as to avoid any continuation of the argument they had had the previous night. Hal groaned quietly at the memory. He rolled over and stuck his feet out over the arm of the sofa while he tried to guess what — if anything — Angelina had left him for breakfast. She usually bought him a selection of croissants and buns as a treat, but perhaps she had been so offended last night that she had stashed them away in the freezer, leaving him to make do with toast or cereal.

A few hours later Hal turned Grace's red Volkswagen Beetle off the motorway and headed toward Thirsk. He liked the car, in spite of the daft little daisy in the vase on the dashboard, although not half as much as the Triumph Spitfire he had sold when he had bought *Calypso*. He had not needed a car once he had the boat, indeed, would not have known where to keep it. He had sailed from one port to another for years, never stopping anywhere for longer than it took to get some work and earn enough money to move on. Whitby had been another of those temporary homes until the day he met Grace. She had put all thoughts of moving on out of his head forever. The money his parents had left him was mostly untouched, but he was glad of it now. He guessed that the near future would probably need some rearranging, if he went ahead with his plan, and extra money would certainly come in handy then. Perhaps he would swap *Calypso* for a bigger boat suitable for a couple … or maybe they could divide their time between *Calypso* and Grace's little flat.

His friend Charlie had been on to him for months to become a full-time partner in the boatyard and maybe start a sideline of building small wooden boats, similar to the traditional Whitby Coble but a little more sophisticated and comfortable. The cobles were designed to be launched off the sloping beaches of the eastern coast and to be sturdy enough to handle well in the frequent storms which regularly hit that coastline. Hal smiled as he contemplated these potential changes in his life. He was ready for change, as long as it involved Grace.

True, before meeting her he had intended to continue to sail around the British coastline for a few more years, then to refit *Calypso* for a round-the-world trip. For that the boat would have needed her chain-plates, rigging and sails updating, but she was a sound vessel with more than three tons of lead fused into her keel which kept her beautifully stable in inclement weather. Hal loved her beautiful lines and had already made a lot of improvements; given the engine a complete overhaul, redone the upholstery and installed gleaming new portholes. He knew that she would have been perfect for the journey in spite of her venerable age. However, a future with Grace seemed no less exciting, and since she loved sailing too, he would not need to choose between the old love and the new. He had no regrets.

He was a little less sure of things than he had been when driving to see his sister though. He kept going back over Angelina's words about him never growing up and not being responsible enough. She had left his mother's ring on the table, along with a fairly decent selection of cakes, so he thought she must have mostly forgiven him for his hurtful comments — but now he kept wondering if giving the ring to Grace was really the great idea it had seemed to him before. What if she *did* expect him to marry her?

He was not ready for that kind of commitment and surely she would not want it either?

Epica blared from the stereo system. He would have played something softer if Grace had been with him, but he loved Simone Simon's voice. He had always had a bit of a crush on her, actually. Redheads in general. Then again, he had fond memories of many different women, but no one had ever moved him the way that Grace did. He smiled as he visualised her compact curves and neat features. He particularly liked the smattering of freckles that darkened her nose, and her laugh. She was so dainty that her laugh came as a shock, being deep and hearty and completely contagious. Hal laughed out loud too and stretched a little. He had made sandwiches before leaving Angelina's, and now his stomach was telling him it was time to eat them. He frowned a little in concentration, wondering if he had tidied Angelina's kitchen to her exacting standards. Probably not — and this time she would probably not forgive him quite so easily after his harsh remarks of the night before. She might not forgive him for using up all of her special *Pâté de Campagne* for his sandwiches, either.

'Blast, I knew I'd forget something,' he said, remembering the sofa. He had left it unmade, the cover on the floor where it had slipped when he had got up and cushions scattered around. That made him feel even worse. Perhaps, as Angelina had said, he really was too selfish and irresponsible.

He worried about his sister sometimes. She never seemed to have much of a life outside of work. She told him about concerts and theatre trips to London, but never seemed to go *with* anyone. She had always been like that — at least …… Hal began to feel guilty again. Angelina had not exactly *said* it was his fault, but clearly, having had to suddenly give up university and look after a younger sibling full-time must have had something to do with it.   Since then, the only person who really got to see the warm and loving person beneath the icy exterior had been Hal himself.   She seemed determined to hide her real self from other people, so no-one had ever got beneath the surface. He couldn't recall her having any close female friends, let alone a male romantic interest. Then again, maybe there was hope for her yet. She had behaved quite differently with Leo Marconi last night. Hal smiled at the idea of the two of them together but did not hold out much hope.

His stomach rumbled. Definitely time to eat. He was almost at Sutton Bank, and shifted down gears to help the car cope with the steep road. At the top was the North Yorkshire Moors Visitor Centre, a place he often stopped at to enjoy the views and walks, if he had time on his way back to Whitby. There was good climbing, too, at the nearby Whitestone Cliffs, which was not for beginners, although he had no time for that today. It would be the perfect place to stop. He had enough time for a short walk, which was exactly what he needed to get his feelings clear and decide whether he really was going to ask Grace to move in with him tonight.

Flashing signs along the road warned him to keep his speed down, and other signs helpfully informed him of how many lorries had been stuck on the tortuous bends there in the course of a year. Luckily there was no one else on the road in front of him today, and Grace's car easily made it up the incline. Hal indicated left and pulled into the visitor centre's car park. He took his sandwich bag and put it into a small rucksack he always kept in the car, adding a large slab of dark chocolate and several energy bars from the emergency rations he stored in the boot. Then he took the rucksack out again, extracted half a cheese sandwich just to be getting on with, and began to chew happily. He shook the flask attached to the rucksack and satisfied himself that it was already full of water.

It was a fairly pleasant summer day. There was a light breeze that sent clouds scudding across the sky, but the intermittent sunshine was warm. Hal folded a waterproof jacket and put it into the pack, and tied a sweatshirt around his waist as well. He knew just how quickly the weather could change here, so would not risk walking in just jeans and T-shirt. He had walking shoes in the boot of the car too but today he intended to have a gentle stroll along a well-trodden path and his trainers would do fine.

He cut in front of the visitor centre, an attractive building of stone, wood and glass, and then turned right toward the Cleveland Way leading to Gormire Lake. His thoughts turned once more to Grace as he fell into a comfortable walking pace. He found walking almost meditative, the fresh air breathed deeply in and out, the natural rhythm of his body and the way his thoughts seemed to calm and clear, no matter what mood he had been in previously. He touched the front pocket of his jeans and reassured himself that the small cloth pouch Angelina had reluctantly left for him was still there. The pouch, containing a pretty ring — an emerald set with small diamonds — had been left on top of a long note written in Angelina's bold script.

'Look after this CAREFULLY' Angelina had warned. *'It would be just like you to put it somewhere and forget where, or drop it off the side of the boat or something!*

You know I kept your mother's jewellery as well as my mother's stuff. I never wear anything of theirs but I like to have it to look at once in a while. I remember that ring on Helen's finger. It made me so angry at first. I could not imagine anyone else taking mother's place but you are so like her, Hal. She won me over just by being herself and never giving up on me. When they died in that crash I felt as if I had lost not only my father but my second mother too.

I have been waiting for the right moment to give you her things. So, this is important to me – take good care of this ring and make sure you really know what you want!

Hal did not remember his mother at all, or his father. He had probably been too young, or maybe he had just blotted out the memories to avoid the pain. Since they had died, Angelina had been both mother and father to him. He was aware that he had been a challenging child.

He had grown up very wild and with a desire to push himself to the limit. Having no parents, just a loving and indulgent sister, he had ignored most of the polite rules of society and done what he felt like. He had certainly put Angelina's love to the test many times over the years, but she had never given up on him either.

He loved the idea of giving this ring to Grace as a sign of inner commitment, and he hoped she would like it, because he wanted somehow to connect his old life with his new one and a new ring would not do that for him. He had always previously believed that marriage was unnecessary and binding, but with Grace he could consider that, maybe, just maybe, it would be a completion. He knew she loved him, but did not think marriage was what she really wanted, either.

There was no one else around, it being a weekday morning and with the ground still quite soggy from recent rain, but that was how Hal liked it. He smiled as the wind picked up and ruffled his hair. Much as he enjoyed the sunshine, a part of him always welcomed extreme weather; it challenged and stimulated him. He loved the wildness of this place, the freedom of being up high and seeing far into the distance with no man-made constructions to spoil the view. Down to the left he could see the dark waters of Lake Gormire through the trees. It was a curious place with no inlet or outflow, extraordinarily beautiful and equally mysterious. Legend had it that the lake was so deep it had no bottom, and he also remembered some story of it being formed when the devil rode his horse over the cliff, the lake springing from the crater that formed when the horse hit the ground. There were all sorts of legends around here, of mythical black stallions and white mares, devil's leaps, strange caves containing skeletons and ancient druid sites. The White Horse of Kilburn was a short walk away, cut into the hillside near Roulston Scar, where Hal occasionally went to watch the gliders overhead.

He was seriously thinking of taking up gliding. There were a lot of similarities between sails and wings. The only thing that was holding him back was the expense of getting a flying licence. He was thinking twice about spending, now that he had Grace to plan his life with. He had found himself watching small children and their mothers recently, and trying, but failing, to imagine having such a responsibility. The whole idea scared him, rather — he wasn't sure he was up to it.

Looking down to the lake he found it hard to believe — especially on such a sunny afternoon — that people had once been so superstitious. Hal had also seen the place under different skies however, with black clouds boiling above and the wind howling along the escarpment so that his climbing group had unanimously decided to call it a day and head for the nearest pub. What was that story Nigel had told them over a drink? — Hal struggled to remember. Something to do with local caves. He knew they had found it hilarious after a couple of pints. Something to do with wind. Now he had it: windypits! The caves were so called because of the noises they made when the wind blew through them. School-boy humour, he thought, a grin spreading across his face.

Pulling his rucksack off his shoulder, Hal retrieved another sandwich to keep his strength up. He shoved the others back into his rucksack, and with the thick slabs of bread in his mouth he wrestled the top off his water flask. Then he took a large bite, chewed, swallowed and had a long drink of water to wash it all down. With the sandwich wedged in his mouth he replaced his water bottle, then took hold of the sandwich again. Just in time, he jumped to one side to avoid a large puddle that had been hidden from him by the slab of bread.

Ahead he saw a good place to stop. A short way off the trail was a flat, grassy slope that edged gently down to boulders and gorse, then another slope before the cliff edge. The views of the lake and moors were stunning, and Hal plonked himself down to enjoy them. Then he swore under his breath. The ground was wetter than it had looked, which was rather unpleasant. Oh well, he would soon dry off once he started walking back. Bringing his hand up to his mouth Hal saw with surprise that he had already finished that sandwich but the hole in his stomach was not full, at all. It was a good job that he had made several. He thought he would try the pâté ones next.

Before he did, though, he wanted to look at his mother's ring once more. Hal shook the ring out into the palm of his hand. It looked ridiculously tiny. He slid it onto the tip of his little finger and admired the way that the diamonds caught the sun. He tried to imagine it on Grace's finger. Was that, in fact, where it belonged? He *still* wasn't sure. As he went to put it back into the pouch, though, it slipped through his fingers and bounced off downhill. Hal really swore now. Not taking his eyes from where he thought the ring had landed, he made his way down the slope. He got down on his hands and knees to get his eyes closer to the ground.

The problem was that the emerald blended in very well with the grass. Hal began to feel worried. He ran his hands over the soft tufts, but with no luck. Sitting back on his haunches he glanced up as a large puffy cloud passed over the sun like a cool touch to his brow. He *had* to find that ring. He could just imagine what Angelina would say to him if he lost it! He started methodically turning his head from one side to the other as he moved slowly forward. Then, as the sun came out again, he saw the diamonds glitter a few inches to his right. Gratefully, Hal picked the ring up and placed it carefully into the pouch, shoving it deep into the front pocket of his jeans. What a relief. His heart was pitter-pattering as he realised how close he had come to losing it.

'Christ, that was a close shave,' he muttered, leaning back against a large boulder to recover.

After a few seconds, now that the danger of losing the ring had passed, Hal's appetite returned. He hauled himself up and plonked his bottom down on the rock, laughing at the memory of his desperate hunt through the tussocks.

So Angelina's prediction had nearly come about. He had nearly lost it through sheer carelessness. Perhaps she knew him better than he thought, and if she was right about this, maybe she was right about Grace as well? Just then the boulder, loosened by the rain, gave way beneath him, and he plummeted into darkness and pain.

7

Grandma Clair's Budgerigar

Grace struggled up the steps outside her house with her shopping bags. Before she had got to the supermarket counter she had been tempted by a box of chocolates and a large bunch of flowers for her grandmother. Now the wine and the sauce jar were making dangerous clinking noises and the irises were slipping from her grip. Plonking the heavy bag down and wincing at the noise of glass on glass, she shoved the flowers under her arm and rummaged in her bag for her keys.

Why was it that, no matter how large or small a handbag was, the one object you wanted at any particular moment sank to the bottom, she wondered? It must be one of those universal laws. Finally she found them and let herself into the entrance hall. She retrieved the chocolates, stuffed the bread between the wine and the sauce jar to separate them, then left her shopping bag by the stairs and knocked on Grandma Clair's door.

A few years ago the townhouse had been divided into three flats. Grace's parents had wanted to move closer to her brother in York and help him out by looking after a growing brood of small grandchildren. Her father, an accountant, had already retired, and her mother was more than happy to leave her office job and become a full time granny. They had kept a flat on the first floor for their regular visits and had transformed the attic into a small but beautifully appointed flat for Grace. Grandma Clair had been adamant that she would not move from Whitby and now lived in the ground floor flat. This was a situation that suited everyone. Grace adored her eccentric grandmother, and felt that she had far more in common with her than with her very down-to-earth parents. Grace's own flat was full of light and she loved the homely feel of the sloping ceilings and white-painted beams. She had a small kitchen and dining area, a bedroom and a bathroom and most importantly, from her front windows, a view of the harbour and *Calypso*.

Knocking on her grandmother's door was for politeness' sake only, since the door was never locked. Now, as Grace entered the flat, with its plants, colourful cushions and piles of magazines and books on every surface, she smiled at the immediate sense of warmth and welcome. Grandma Clair called out from the kitchen at the back of the flat, 'Come on in, child.' At the same time the loud screech of an old-fashioned steam kettle greeted her, followed by a hoarse command of '*Wipe your feet*!' Grandma Clair had not had a steam kettle for years; the noise emanated from her pet budgerigar.

The flat smelt sugary-sweet. Grandma was making strawberry jam, Grace saw, as she brushed past a large Swiss-cheese plant and went into the kitchen. Through the window the garden displayed bright blooms that were repeated in pots and vases all around the flat. Grace had inherited many things from her grandmother, but unfortunately green fingers was not one of them.

'Hi Grandma,' Grace said, kissing her cheek, then tickled the budgerigar under its beak the way it liked.

'Good evening, Thatcher,' she said, twisting her own head on one side in response to the bird's scrutiny.

'*Pretty, pretty Thatcher,*' replied the bird and then, rather disconcertingly, began to purr like a cat as it nestled closer to Grandma Clair's neck, small claws sinking into the old lady's home-made purple cardigan. Thatcher was named after the former Prime Minister, not because Grandma had approved of the Iron Lady's politics but because she was a woman who excelled in a man's world and whose redoubtable spirit Grandma Clair had admired. Unfortunately the bird had turned out to be a male, so the feminine Margaret had been swapped for gender-neutral Thatcher. He hardly ever went into his cage, preferring to sit on Grandma Clair's shoulder or perch on her knitting needles. That may well have been the reason why the many garments produced by the busy needles were often so shapeless.

The old lady kept stirring her jam but flapped a hand in the direction of the table, where a pot of tea and two cups sat waiting. Her grandmother always knew when

Grace would arrive, and what kind of tea she would need to lift her mood or warm her up. Tea in the afternoons, but in the morning they would drink the special blend of Jamaican Blue Mountain coffee that Grandma ordered specially.

Placing the irises in the sink, Grace put the chocolates at the end of the table then pulled out a chair and sat, suddenly realising how tired she was. All afternoon she had been dogged by a headache in the quiet moments between customers. Her usual remedy of a drop of lavender essential oil rubbed into her temples had not worked. She picked up the teapot and poured. Today's tea was gingery and spicy, Grace noticed as she gratefully inhaled. Chosen with energy and romance in mind? And at this thought, she smiled dreamily.

Grandma Clair turned to look over her shoulder and smiled fondly back at Grace. Despite the difference in age, there was a remarkable resemblance between the two of them, in particular the sprinkling of freckles over their well-shaped noses, although Grace's skin was a shade lighter.

'Grace, child, I saw a ring in my tea-leaves this morning. Have you got anything to tell me?' she asked. Grace, looking at the purple, budgerigar-decorated shoulders, felt a surge of intense love for her grandmother. She was twenty-nine, but knew she would always be *child* for her grandma. She also knew that the old lady could not wait for her to get married so that she could have some more great-grandchildren to spoil, but it was more than a general hope that had inspired Grandma's remark.

'Stop that, Grandma,' she replied with an indulgent smile. 'It takes all the fun out of life when you do that. I'd prefer to be surprised, if it's going to happen.'

She was so used to Grandma Clair's ways that she felt no surprise at the question. Clairvoyance was one of the things she had inherited, although her gift manifested itself somewhat differently and she preferred to keep quiet about it to people she did not know well. Her grandmother, on the other hand, did not care what anyone thought. Grace's father had always been deeply suspicious and embarrassed by his mother, and was far happier in the company of his pragmatic lawyer son than that of his daughter, who had showed worrying signs of being similarly 'unusual' from an early age. Grace's mother had struggled even more to accept her family's eccentricities. A good Catholic girl fresh from Ireland when she had met John Williams, she was constantly torn between love for her child and fear of what forces were at work within her. She avoided her mother-in-law as much as possible and preferred to think of the old woman as a harmless crackpot rather than anything potentially more disturbing.

'Her wits were addled when her husband died,' was her usual explanation of any odd behaviour manifested in public.

Grandma Clair declared the jam to be ready and began to ladle it into the jars arrayed on the worktop by the hob. A large blob missed a jar and plopped onto the floor, making the old lady hiss with annoyance.

'*Whoops-a-daisy*,' said Thatcher, making them laugh. Grandma Clair refused Grace's offer of help with the jam, but asked her to pour some tea.

'Making jam sure is thirsty work'. The Caribbean lilt made her voice musical, and Grace loved to listen to her talk. So did Thatcher. He whistled *Jamaica Farewell*, the tune that Grandpa Jimmy had taught him, into the old lady's ear and was rewarded with a sticky jam finger to nibble at.

Grace had lovely memories of her grandfather. He had seemed to her to be always laughing, and she had loved to stand on his feet as he danced her around the room singing '*Had to leave a little girl in Kingston town,*' while Grandma Clair had pretended not to notice his flirting. Grandma Clair was his own 'little girl from Kingston town' but he had not left her behind when he took up the British government's invitation to its overseas colonies to come and work in England. Instead, he had married her and they had travelled together to a new life in a draughty and wet country. He always joked that no matter how miserable the weather, his Clair kept him warm.

Grandma Clair kept the cushions plumped up in his armchair and no one else was ever allowed to sit there. However, her Grandmother did not miss him as much as she might have. Grandma Clair talked to him and other friendly spirits throughout the day. She said she was never lonely because there was always someone to chat with. Grace occasionally smelt her grandfather's clean soap and talc scent in the air, but since the same soap had been used in the house forever, this was not conclusive evidence that his presence was really there. Grandma Clair had no doubts, though.

Grace absentmindedly fingered the delicate gold crucifix she always wore around her neck, a present from her grandparents on her eighteenth birthday, and thought wistfully of her Grandpa. Her Grandma involved her dead husband and other spirit friends in her daily life as often as she invoked Jesus, and asked for his intervention in many minor matters, from helping a wilted plant recover, to getting the jam to set properly. The walls of the apartment were covered in photos of her loved ones, interspersed with religious knick-knacks. There was a pretty plastic Madonna on the windowsill in the bathroom, and postcards of saints and Jesus tucked behind mirrors. Over Grandma Clair's bed hung a particular favourite, an intricate gilded icon showing Jesus with a beautifully soulful expression, which Grace had bought back from a holiday in Romania a few years previously.

Jam finished, Grandma Clair washed her hands and exclaimed over the irises, finding a vase under the sink and arranging them swiftly. She placed the flowers on the table and kissed Grace's cheek before sitting down and sipping her tea with obvious pleasure. She poured a drop into her saucer, and Thatcher hopped from her shoulder on to the table for his afternoon treat. Grace passed the biscuit tin over, and smiled at the familiar ritual of a digestive being halved. One half was dunked in the tea cup and chewed, the other was crumbled in the saucer and pecked at.

'So, what does Grandpa think about Hal?' Grace asked, plucking a biscuit crumb from the front of the old lady's purple cardigan. Her grandmother felt the cold. She dreamt of the balmy days of her youth, kept the temperature high inside her flat and wore one of her ghastly knitted creations all year round. As far as Grandma Clair was concerned the more colourful the better. As she had come in, Grace had spotted the latest woollen concoction on the sofa in front of the TV. Grandma Clair had recently discovered multi-coloured wool, this time in red, pink and orange. Grace hoped that it would not be a Christmas gift for her.

Settling back in her chair Grandma Clair pursed her lips and looked thoughtfully at Grace, considering her words carefully.

'Well darling, you know your grandfather and his funny ideas. It would be hard for him to accept that anyone is good enough for his little girly but,' she started to laugh and reached up to her own shoulder as if patting an invisible hand, 'but, he says Hal is a good man. He's a little wild yet but his heart is in the right place. All Grandpa wants is for you to be happy.'

Her grandmother reached across and stroked Grace's cheek now.

'That's what we both want for you, Gracie. Now, hadn't you better stop hanging around with us old folks and get yourself prettied up for that man, eh?'

Grace looked at her watch and jumped up. Grandma was right: if she wanted to have a shower and choose something pretty to wear before dinner she had better hurry. She kissed her grandmother goodbye and tickled Thatcher.

As she left the kitchen, the steam kettle whistled again and Thatcher reminded her to wipe her feet. She laughed quietly as she crossed the living room but, just as she reached out for the door handle it was as if a cloud suddenly swept across her sun. She turned and groped blindly for her Grandma's armchair as darkness swept through her. She was aware of a supporting arm and Grandma Clair's voice near her ear as she helped her to sit, telling her to let go and relax.

'Don't fight it darling, let it come. You're safe. I'm here,'

The words faded, the gentle stroking pressure on her arm did too and Grace gasped with fear. *So much pain. She was in a cold, dark space. Hal was there, she knew, but she could not reach him. His mind was closed, so far away. Even the terrible pain that he had felt, which he had sent into her mind, was dimmed. She could not reach him, could not wake him.*

Grace came back to herself slowly, reluctant to break even this tenuous link with Hal. Grandma Clair was crooning softly to her, stroking her hair, and Thatcher was gently nibbling her ear. Her cheeks were cold with tears and she was trembling. Grandma wrapped a brightly coloured knitted patchwork blanket around her and took hold of her hands.

'Tell me about it, child,' she urged.

8

In the middle
of the journey of our life ...

Angelina poured herself a glass of the expensive Italian wine she had bought on impulse earlier that week, tempted from her usual French Cuvée by wondering what Mr Marconi would have chosen. She appreciated the colour in the flawless Dartington crystal and the smooth, rich flavour as she sipped. She didn't drink much but enjoyed the little luxuries in life. That reminded her that Hal had eaten all the delicious *pâté* she had been looking forward to, darn the man. She wasn't really irritated though. It hadn't taken her long to clear his crumbs from the kitchen and straighten the sofa. She loved seeing her crazy brother and especially seeing him so happy.

As she prepared radishes to add to a fresh salad she pondered this new phenomenon of 'Hal in love' and shook her head. She was glad for him. He would be a good, faithful partner for the right lady and had so much warmth to give.

Unlike her - Hal had been right about that, she admitted.

She heated a pan and slid a steak in to cook quickly, nice and rare. As she waited she was aware of the silence, apart from the meat as it hissed in the pan. Not wanting to face dreams caused by nostalgic musical choices and unable to select the right classical music for her mood she had decided to do without but, after Hal's visit, she felt rather alone tonight. Angelina usually enjoyed being alone and she hardly ever felt lonely but tonight she was unsettled.

She was good at her job and at matching people and homes but Mr Marconi was proving a real challenge. Sitting down to eat, Angelina amused herself by thinking about her clients that day, two time-wasters, a nit-picker, a ninny, and a mummy's boy she thought, scathingly, dismissing them. That was the best thing about her job, she could be efficient in the office and leave all thoughts of work behind when she left. Except for Mr Marconi. She was seriously wondering what else she could show him and even Julie hadn't offered any helpful gems.

Julie was surprisingly quick and sometimes Angelina thought that the office would do better in her hands. She had a knack of making people feel good. Angelina could see people visibly relax when Julie came over to talk. Like the newlyweds who had been in last week looking for a first home. She had been hugely pregnant, had hardly fitted into the chair. Angelina had suggested a small new-build home not far from the centre of town and had remarked on the nursery school around the corner, which has solicited smiles and head nods. Then Julie had plonked herself on the edge of the desk and started chattering, as if she had known these people forever,

'Oh yeah, that's right Miss Snow. *Little Pickles* it's called. Rosie White, who I was at school with, works there. She's lovely and she says the kids really love it there. That would be really handy for you, wouldn't it?'

The couple had been convinced and Angelina knew that it was Julie's enthusiasm and local knowledge that had made the sale.

After washing up and cleaning the kitchen Angelina corked the bottle of red, surprised to see that she had drunk two glasses instead of her usual one. Maybe that was why she felt restless. She settled on the sofa and reached for a book from the pile on the coffee table. 'The Divine Comedy', Marconi had mentioned that book to her and she had bought a copy to see why he liked it so much. She flicked through the introduction and began to read, 'In the middle of the journey of our life I found myself within a dark wood where the straight way was lost.'

She struggled on for a few more pages and then gave up and picked up a modern murder/mystery instead. Much better. At least she didn't have to struggle with complicated metaphors, just some rather grisly descriptions. That book lasted a whole chapter before being put back on the pile. She crossed to the window and drew the curtains aside. No rain tonight. A few stars showing dimly in the slit of sky visible between roof tops.

For some reason Dante's words had got to her. She thought about Mr Marconi's morose face. He was older than her but they were both well and truly in the middle of their journey through life. She had not often felt lost on that journey, at least not since she was a child. What was the matter with her tonight, why all these unwanted insights?

She turned on the TV - Strictly Come Dancing - turned it off again. Paced around the room. She picked up her mobile phone and dialled Hal's number but there was no reply. Thank goodness for that or he would think she was checking up on him and, being highly perceptive when it came to her, he would probably have sensed that she was not in a good mood.

For some reason she hesitated, finger hovering over the entry for Marconi L. She drew an irritated breath and pressed the button. Marconi answered too quickly and she practically barked down the phone, telling him she had another place to show him, if he was free the next morning.

'Of course, dear lady. It would be a pleas ...'.

She cut him off midsentence, informed him curtly to meet her at the office at 11am and hung up. She would find the right home for him and get him out of her life as quickly as possible, she vowed as she climbed into bed and tried to get comfortable.

9

Unlikely Travelling Companions

'I am a non-smoker, don't you know, old chap,' Leonardo informed the face in the mirror, in his best British accent. His reflection did not look convinced. The desire for a cigarette had been nagging at him since he had woken up. Only the thought of Angelina Snow, wrinkling her nose with disgust at the faintest whiff of smoke on him, had enabled him to remain strong. In spite of the unruly sprouts of hair that stood up on his head, the stubbled chin and the deep bags under his eyes, Leo was quite pleased with his reflection. He looked much brighter than he had for years. The anger, pain and disillusionment that had been his constant companions before his little swim in the Tevere River had diminished. The cynical armour he had created to defend his wounded soul was indelibly etched into the craggy lines of his face, but there was a hint of humour in his eyes and he felt almost sprightly as he reached for the razor and began to get ready for his appointment with Miss Snow.

He was glad to have a Saturday morning appointment this time. Maybe she would be more relaxed on a weekend and he could convince her to have lunch with him. Or maybe he would ask if she was free for dinner.

'*Accidenti*!' he swore, reverting to Italian as he nicked his chin with the razor blade. He had better concentrate instead of indulging himself by imagining those long legs stretched out on his sofa, the skirt riding up just a little as she sipped coffee and prepared to launch one of her sharp, sarcastic quips at him.

Half an hour later, Leo was sauntering along Bourne High Street wearing his favourite yellow pullover and carrying his rain jacket over one arm, just in case. Everyone else was dressed for an English July. There were sandals, T-shirts and shorts everywhere, in spite of the scudding clouds and the distinct chill in the air. The fact that the sun had come out for the first time in weeks had incited a general madness in the local population, Leo decided, as two extremely large ladies passed by, wearing tight vest-tops and leggings. He shuddered and thought longingly of the typical Roman beauty, all swaying curves and dark hair bouncing over tanned shoulders, and looking indefinably stylish in whatever she wore, no matter her age or size. Leo sometimes wondered what he was doing here, in this country that his Roman ancestors had conquered and then abandoned

— more than likely because of the weather, he thought. There was a delightful expression that a French friend had told him years ago when talking about weather in his native Normandy: *S'il ne pleut pas il va plevoir* which roughly translated as *If it is not raining now it is about to*. Leo, having lived in England for some time now, in what should have been the spring and summer, felt that he could add to that. If it was not raining, it was icy cold enough to snow, and if it was not doing either of those things there was fog.

Or then again, maybe the Roman army had left because of the unimaginative food and badly dressed locals. The Roman's best togas and sandals would not only have been cold, but wasted on those with such a distinct lack of sartorial elegance. Not everyone was as badly dressed as the two large ladies, but the only suntans to be seen were the spray type on young girls, who for some reason appeared to believe that orange skin was sexy.

***

Pondering the many and various eccentricities he had encountered on British soil, Leo added to the list the impossibility of finding a simple plumbing solution for a leaky toilet cistern in his bachelor annex. The complexities of the system beneath the ceramic lid and the fact that everything in the hardware store was gauged in inches had made him give up and send for a local plumber to fix it. After several *'nice cups of tea'* and a heated discussion about the football season, the toilet had been fixed and Leo and Barry were getting along splendidly, but when Leo had thought to ask about substituting his hot and cold taps with a mixer, his new friend had looked bemused and wondered why he would want to do such a thing. The final proof that Brits were indeed barbaric was the total absence of the bidet, Leo concluded. They were apparently non-existent in either homes or shops. Cousin Luigi loved to tell the story of the time, years ago, when he had ordered a bidet to be sent from Italy, and had called a plumber to fit it. When he had come home a few hours later he had found it installed on the wall as a urinal.

Leo wondered what Angelina would be wearing. She was the only reason he was still here, now that he had recovered from his operation in the noisy, welcoming bosom of his family. Nothing feminine for work, of course. Yesterday evening's silky dress had been quite a revelation. It had been the first time he had seen her legs properly since the day they had lured him into the office.

How that woman intrigued him! Leo wondered sometimes if the aneurysm had caused a kind of madness or a personality change. He was seeing ghosts and was completely besotted by a woman who held the whole world at arm's length. Apart from her brother, Leo amended: with him she had been a different woman. Leo knew it was perverse, but the haughty, cold persona that made most people feel uncomfortable with Miss Snow was the thing that had most attracted him to her, because he understood only too well the need to alienate oneself from others.

He had worked for years behind the scenes in his cubbyhole office, gathering news items and information for the Associated Press and putting it onto computers, having very little contact with anyone except his office colleagues. He had managed to keep even those at a distance, with his abrupt manner and impatience, until he was generally considered by them to be completely unsociable. After work he would shut himself away in his room at home to avoid contact with his mother, or drive to the boat and spend the night there. He knew all there was to know about building walls to keep others out, he was a champion wall-builder, and he recognised a kindred spirit in Angelina Snow.

What had changed now was that for the first time in his life he had an urge to break down those walls, both his own and Angelina's. The question was …. how to do that. Last night he had glimpsed the warmth that lay within her, if he could just find the key. The most important thing, he decided, was to take it slowly. One brick at a time, he told himself, just the way Rome had been built. Also, to be strong and determined and not give up when she rebuffed him, which was inevitably going to happen, he decided.

He was almost at the office when a black Audi A4 pulled up and parked outside. As the door opened he realised that the driver was Angelina herself. He recognised the legs that slid out, ending in red stilettos that stabbed the pavement. Oh, this was going to be a *wonderful* day!

Miss A. Snow was adequately dressed for the weather, wearing a red pencil skirt and a short-sleeved navy blouse, with a navy cardigan thrown across the handles of her matching handbag. Leo forced down the smile that threatened to overwhelm his face and greeted her with a simple 'Good morning, Miss Snow.'

She swivelled on those marvellous heels and nodded curtly.

'Mr Marconi. On time today, I see. Are you *sure* you need a pullover in this weather?' One dark eyebrow arched up as she eyed the offending garment, and Leonardo settled back happily on his heels, stared bravely up to meet her eyes with his best gloomy expression. and replied that if she could wear those heels he was entitled to his pullover. He detected a small twitch in her cheek — which could have been a suppressed smile — but she turned her back on him immediately and gestured to the passenger seat.

'The house I want to show you today is about a ten-minute drive. Shall we get on?'

'Of course, dear lady, if you can drive in those shoes,' Leo replied, getting in and breathing in the pleasant scent of new leather. Angelina folded herself elegantly behind the steering wheel and he watched her slim ankles above the red shoes manoeuvre themselves into position over the pedals.

Before she could start the engine, however, her mobile phone rang and she delved into her handbag for it and answered with a brisk 'Snow speaking.'

The rest of the conversation was one-sided, from Mr Marconi's point of view, with Angelina making small noises first of encouragement and then concern. Something was wrong. Angelina had become so still and focussed that the air in the car seemed to crackle.

'Maybe it's nothing, he's always getting into scrapes,' she said once; but her hands tightened on the phone as she continued to listen.

The voice at the other end suddenly got louder, and Leo heard a woman's voice saying, 'You don't understand, I *saw* him, cold and hurt. I'm afraid.' Then the volume was lowered again and all he could hear was a murmur and Angelina's shallow breathing.

At the end of the call Leo was surprised at how gentle Angelina's voice sounded as she said, 'OK, Grace. I understand. Try not to worry. I will be there as soon as I can.'

Angelina hung up and swivelled to look at him.

'I am sorry, Leonardo, we will have to reschedule our appointment. I need to go to Whitby. Hal is missing. That was his girlfriend on the phone and she sounded very worried.'

She pushed her hand through her hair, messing up its precise lines without realising, and Leo repressed an urge to smooth it for her.

'It is probably just one of his usual scrapes and he will turn up safe and sound, having had a marvellous adventure, just as soon as I have made the trek up there.'

Things were definitely serious, Leo thought. Not only had she forgotten to call him Mr Marconi, she had also lost her haughty look, and he felt an overwhelming desire to put his arms around her and comfort her. Instead, he opened the car door and got out, saying that it was no problem and he would ring her the following week.

***

As she drove off, Leo stood watching, and cursing himself for not being more helpful. He squeezed his nose with his fingers and frowned, then, having come to an important decision, he set off for home as quickly as he could. Once there, Leo sprinted up his path, let himself into the annex, and opened the inner door that linked it to the rest of the house, shouting loudly for his nephew. He then swiftly grabbed a few necessary items and stuffed them into a leather bag with a sturdy shoulder strap. Marco stuck his head around the door looking alarmed.

'What's up, *Zio*?' he asked. Leo had no desire to explain the situation and merely asked if Marco knew Angelina Snow's address.

'I know where she lives, yes. Why?'

Leo ignored the question.

'Will you take me there, now?' he requested, and Marco, looking resigned, nodded and picked up his uncle's bag. It was surprisingly heavy.

'Whatever have you got in there?' he queried.

'Let's see,' Leo said. As he listed the items he had packed, he mentally checked that he had indeed got everything he would need for a day or two.

'Pyjamas, one spare shirt, one pair of boxers, one pair of socks, my toothbrush and deodorant and four bottles of Montalcino ...' He dashed back into his bedroom shouting over his shoulder, 'Knew I had forgotten something,' and reappeared with his beloved Wave pocket-knife that he never travelled without. It had blades for everything, and most important of all, a nifty little corkscrew.

Marco shook his head at his uncle's eccentric ways and carried the bag to his car. He tried once more to find out what Leonardo was up to, knowing that the rest of the family would want to know later.

'So, where are you going, *Zio*?'

'On a trip to somewhere, to find someone,' was the enigmatic reply.

'You make it sound like some kind of pilgrimage,' Marco said with a huge smile, and Leonardo laughed and patted his nephew's shoulder.

'Just so, my boy,' he replied. 'I think you are right. I am on a journey into the unknown territory of the heart, a veritable quest!'

***

Angelina rarely dithered but she was clearly dithering now. Her open suitcase on the bed already contained several colour-coordinated outfits that were both elegant and comfortable. There were two pairs of shoes in a canvas bag by the bed. Then she remembered her stay on Hal's boat and how hot under the collar he had got over her footwear, angrily exclaiming, 'Those are *not* boat shoes, Lili!' So she took out one pair of high heels and substituted a pair of soft suede loafers, which on second thoughts she slipped on her feet straight away, because they would be good for driving in. Then she rummaged in her wardrobe until she found a hardly-used pair of jeans, and cursed her brother and his selfish escapades. All the other dratted boat rules flooded back to her and made her hiss angrily.

NEVER JUMP ON DECK

NEVER GO BAREFOOT, *unless you want a broken foot.*

BE VERY CAREFUL WITH THE WATER. *You can brush your teeth with a small glass of water – do not run the tap!*

And then there was Hal's favourite: ONLY COMB YOUR HAIR OUTSIDE ON DECK AND DOWN-WIND.

No wonder she did not like boats much!

Hal was forever getting into trouble, and then she would have to bail him out. Ever since he was a baby she had been rescuing him from one escapade or another. If it had not been for the obvious worry in Grace's voice (and what a nice, warm voice she had) she would not be rushing off now. He would undoubtedly be back on his blasted boat before she had got past Lincoln.

Angelina stopped for a second and sat on the bed, trying to slow her racing heart. Every time Hal was in trouble she would get angry so that she would not have to feel the frantic worry that threatened to tear her apart. She remembered creeping past him the previous morning, refraining from bending to kiss him while he slept, and being overwhelmed by memories. She had learnt during his teenage years to steal kisses while he slept; she had learnt to stand back and wait for the rare bear-hugs. She had so missed the spontaneous cuddles of his childhood. Watching him sleep, so young and yet almost a man, with limbs hanging off the bed and his hair squashed into a crest, she would kiss his warm cheek and sneak out of his room again.

Grace had said that she'd had a *feeling* that Hal was injured. She said that she had these sensations and had learnt to pay attention to them. It all sounded a bit peculiar to Angelina, but she admitted to herself that there had been something in Grace's tone that had unsettled her. The woman had been so adamant that Hal was in trouble that, for some reason, Angelina had believed her.

Enough of getting worked up; it was not helping at all. She stood up, turned back to the contents of her case and tried to hurry up. It was not easy for her to hurry packing a case though, no matter how urgent it was. There were two distinct sides to Angelina, the one she showed to the world, elegantly wrapped in designer clothes and signature heels; and the comfortable woman safe in her own home who wore over-sized slippers and brushed-cotton pyjamas. Then there was the *boat factor*, or in other words having to take something with her which she would not mind becoming ripped, stained and impregnated with the disagreeable odour of damp and engine oil.

She came to the underwear drawer. No difficulty of choice here, anyway. She adored sensual silk and lace against her skin, and her last pair of big knickers had belonged to her school gym-kit. She moved on to the pyjama drawer. Remembering all too well how any part of her body not well clad in a thick insulating layer immediately developed the most spectacular bruises in Hal's front cabin, she reached for the oldest pair.

Just then the doorbell rang. She looked at her watch. It was 12.30 and she was not expecting anyone. She strode down the hallway and opened the door, then stared down in utter surprise at Mr Marconi, still wearing his yellow pullover and carrying a small leather bag over one shoulder as well as his rain-jacket.

'I thought you needed company,' he said with a totally disarming smile. She shook her head, but he had already walked past her into the flat and was admiring the books in the living room.

'*This* is the kind of house I would like. Why haven't you shown me anything like this?' he said accusingly, bending to examine the books on the bottom shelves. 'Why don't I make us coffee and a snack, and then we won't have to stop on the way to Whitby,' he continued in a most reasonable voice.

'Mr Marconi, I am quite all right, I do not want to eat, and there is absolutely no way that you are coming with me,' Angelina said more loudly than she had intended to. She lowered her voice and tried again. 'Thank you for your concern, but I am quite capable of —'

'My dear,' he cut in. 'I have no doubt whatsoever about your capabilities, but I can see that you are shaking. You need to eat before you set off, and you also need to calm down.' Without waiting for her to reply, he set off towards the kitchen and there began to open the fridge and rummage in cupboards.

Angelina started to say something, but suddenly realised that he was right: her hands *were* shaking and she did not feel anywhere near as composed as she needed to be. She had been fine until that wretched man arrived, but then her innate honesty kicked in and she corrected herself. She was genuinely worried about Hal and had got herself into a state. Mr Marconi was being far kinder than a stranger had any obligation to be. Angelina went to finish packing, accompanied by the sound of coffee percolating and pans being vigorously clanged.

Angelina stuffed some night-clothes into the case and added on top of these a large grey cashmere cardigan and two pairs of socks. Then, of course the case would not shut, even when sat on, so she dumped the jeans and some other garments at random into the canvas holdall containing her shoes. Mr Marconi was whistling in the kitchen, a rather good *Va Pensiero – damn* the man.

She dumped her luggage by the door, smoothed down the dove-grey jersey top over loose-fitting black linen trousers that she had changed into for the journey, and frowned at Mr Marconi who was waving the coffee pot at her from the kitchen. She sat at her table feeling like a guest in her own home, and sipped the coffee.

'Too weak!' she exclaimed.

'I quite agree, but I didn't want you to start shaking again. Here, eat your cheese sandwich, Angelina,' he continued. The way his deep voice pronounced her name with a slight Italian intonation sent a flood of warmth through her, and Angelina concentrated her attention on the toasted sandwich to avoid meeting his glance. It was delicious, and she began to feel better and more like herself. He was humming now, completely at home. He had her copy of Jerome K. Jerome's *Three Men in a Boat* by his plate.

'Absolutely my favourite book,' he informed her. 'I have it in Italian, English, French and German. I practise the languages with it. When I can understand the humour in each language I have got to a good point. Also, Montmorency is my kind of dog!'

Angelina was suddenly very glad that he was there. Not that she would admit it to him, of course. He put his cup down.

'So, shall we go?' he asked. She nodded and smiled as they moved in synchronised movements to pick up plates and cups and take them to the sink. She washed, he dried. Then, without more ado, Mr Marconi made for the door and opened it for her, waving her through. Before she could protest, he had taken his bag and her case – good job it had wheels: as it was almost as big as he was. Angelina found the contrast oddly touching.

10

A Presence in the Dark

The pain in his head came and went in waves but there was a constant dull ache throughout his body. Hal struggled to hold on to his lucidity this time. He had felt himself awakening several times, but as soon as he had tried to move, a rush of pain had sent him plummeting back into darkness.

In fact darkness was the most overwhelming sensation he had. He had not been able to understand if it was in his mind or really surrounding him, pressing down on his chest and seeping into his skin. He had no idea how much time has passed since he had fallen. *Into a bloody windypit, of all the ridiculous things!* He started to laugh, and then wished he hadn't, because his head throbbed with the movement. He lay still and tried to make some sense of where he was. There was a very slight lessening of the darkness, and above him he could make out a vague shimmer that he eventually understood to be light filtering through a small gap high up. Probably that had been the space he had fallen through when the rock covering it had given way, and it had been almost refilled by other sliding mud and debris. The light was too dim for him to make out the proportions of the space in which he lay, or to see his body, which made him feel eerily unreal. He slowly tried to move, bringing his hands up to touch his face. He noticed a sticky wetness at one side of his forehead as he gently probed, and he winced. He must have hit his head hard if it had left him unconscious for what seemed ages. He tried moving his legs next, and that was when real panic set in. His legs would not obey. Maybe he was paralysed, oh God, please don't let me be paralysed! His heart stampeded in his chest and his breath jerked wildly.

'Stay still, lad. Thy legs are not hurt, only covered by the earth brought down with thee. That was some mighty fall. No doubt thy body hurts most wretchedly.'

'Shit! Who's there?' Hal yelled, his voice hoarse in his dusty throat, scared almost out of his wits by the whispering voice so close to his face. He strained his eyes to see but it was no use, everything was shades of darkness. Whoever had spoken to him made no effort to help. Maybe he was buried too, Hal thought. He began to move his legs again, wriggling them gently until he felt the heavy earth shift slightly. He pushed himself slowly into a sitting position, waves of nausea threatening to send him back into unconsciousness, then gradually pushed the mud and stones away to free his legs.

'Are you OK? Do you need help?' he asked and was rewarded by the sound of soft laughter.

'Nay, lad. There is no help *you* can give *me*, but maybe some I can give thee. Be stout of heart and I will guide thee, if the good Lord wish it so,' said the soft, disembodied voice. It was a strange sound, the accent strong and unfamiliar to Hal. It sounded northern but not like the local accents he was used to. There was something old-fashioned about it, and he had the impression that the man was very old and maybe not completely sane. Some not very pleasant thoughts ran through his mind. *Christ! The revenge of the windypits. That will teach me to take God's name in vain. Stuck down a windypit with a madman – great!*

Well, it was time to pull himself together. He began to take stock of the situation. Reaching behind him, he slipped his rucksack off his shoulders. As he moved, the pain in his back became savage and he sat a moment cradling the rucksack until his ragged breathing stilled. He was well aware of how lucky he had been. In some unbelievably fortunate way, the rucksack had shielded him and acted as a buffer between him and the boulder he had fallen on. His back was bruised and cut, but the rucksack had taken the brunt of the impact. He fumbled with the latches and delved into the bag until his fingers found the flashlight. Huge relief flooded through him as he pressed the switch and found it still worked. The relief was swiftly forgotten as the seriousness of his situation became apparent. The weak beam illuminated smooth rock walls that would be impossible to climb, and the dim light above was far too high for him to hope to reach it. There was no sign of the old man, but there was the black mouth of another cave to his left; maybe he had gone in there?

***

Hal contemplated the torch. He would have to use it carefully and make the batteries last as long as possible. He located his water bottle and rinsed his mouth out, spitting out dirt with relief. Then he took a small sip and swallowed. He would have to ration that too. Next he checked his phone, which had been in the back pocket of his jeans. It was clear at once that he wasn't going to be able to raise the alarm with it. The screen was smashed, and there was no reaction when he tried to activate it. He shoved it in his rucksack and felt around for the sandwiches. They too had been squashed by the impact but he decided to eat them anyway, leaving the chocolate and energy bars for later. If he was going to find a way out of this, he needed some energy fast. He was also cold, from shock and the unpleasantly dank air, so pulled on his sweatshirt and waterproof jacket, feeling immediately comforted.

He turned off the flashlight, shoved it in his pocket and ate in the dark. As he munched the soggy pâté and bread, not hungry for maybe the first time in his life, he thought of his sister and felt a lump in his throat. She would be worried when he did not ring to tell her he was home. Angry with him too, he thought. Hal, in trouble again! Then his thoughts turned to Grace. He had a vague memory of hearing her voice in the darkness just after he had fallen. Wishful thinking, he supposed. At least he knew that she would come looking for him — and Angelina too once she knew he was missing. There was no doubt that very soon people would be searching for him. The problem was that no one knew *where* to look — and who would imagine looking down a windypit? No, if he wanted to get out of here he would have to rely on himself, and that meant exploring his surroundings better and taking a look at that other cave where there just … *might* be an escape route.

'Gather your strength and follow me now,' breathed the old man's voice. Hal jumped and regretted it at once when his head began to throb fiercely again. There was no scent in the air of another person and he had not heard any noise. No scrape of shoes on the ground, no rustle of fabric. He fumbled the flashlight out of his pocket and flashed the light around the cave. No one. Hal felt the hairs on his arms stand upright. He realised that he was probably still in shock and that the blow to his head might have dimmed his senses, but the man should have been visible. There was no way he could have moved into the dark passageway so quickly and so silently, and yet, when the voice came again, it sounded as if the old man was over there.

'Ready, lad?' the old man asked, his voice quiet and reassuringly real.

'Who are you?' Hal asked.

''Tis of no importance.   But thou, young intruder, dost thou have a name?'

For some reason Hal replied with his full name, something he had not done since school, and a dry cackle of mirth exploded from the darkness.

'Halliwell Snow, Well, well,' the disembodied voice said. 'I see that I have been sent a knight with a pure heart. A clear enough sign, thank the Lord. Come, Halliwell, bring thy light here and find the path thou seekest. "Seek, and you shall find", you know.'

11

A Luscious Lunch

Julie straightened the diary and lined up multi-coloured pens in a row. She balanced a paperclip on each pen, then began to see how high a pile she could make before they fell. She examined her nails - one of the Union Jacks had a chip. She would phone Trisha and see if she could pop in on the way home. What colour should she try next?

It was no good, she was bored and even thinking about her nails wasn't doing the trick. She had nothing to do. She was up to date with all the filing, the office was perfectly spic and span, the phone hadn't rung in over an hour, she had made all the calls on her list and cancelled Miss Snow's appointments for the next couple of days, as requested.

She had never heard her boss in a state like that, shouting garbled instructions down the phone. All Julie had really understood was that Handsome Hal had got into some kind of a trouble so Miss Snow was dashing off to find him and might be gone for a couple of days. She had seen Miss Snow drive up and greet Mr Marconi that morning, then shortly afterwards speed off alone, leaving the Italian man on the pavement, staring after her with an odd look on his face. Julie suspected the sweet man had a bit of a crush on her boss, which amused her no end. He had no chance, of course, but what a funny looking couple they would make.

Thinking about having a crush on someone reminded her of Marco, Leonardo's nephew from the restaurant. Julie had a rather *large* crush on him and she thought he might like her too. Hal was gorgeous but she knew very well that she wasn't his type. Marco though ... well, it *was* lunch time and a girl had to eat. She fancied a bit of Italian, and Miss Snow wouldn't be back today so she could have a nice long lunch break. Before she hung the *back soon* notice on the door, Julie pulled the red band off her plait and ran a brush through her thick blonde hair, then she applied red lipstick and undid another button on her blouse. That should do the trick.

Ten minutes later Julie was at the best table in *Il Toscano*, studying the menu Marco had given her. She was glad he had sat her near the window so that the sun would make her hair glow nicely. She'd have a glass of prosecco and a plate of whatever the handsome Italian suggested, she decided, watching him weaving through the tables toward her.

'La bella Julie, what would you like?' he asked with a charming smile. As he reached to take her menu back she saw part of a tattoo where his shirt sleeve had ridden up.

'Oh, I like that. I'd like one here,' she said, pulling her blouse off her shoulder to show the top of her arm.

***

Who would have thought that the sight of plump white skin and pink bra strap could have this effect on a man's pulse? To add to that pleasure was the fact that Julie had quite obviously anticipated his reaction. She smiled up at him and asked for the special. Marco struggled to concentrate on the order instead of the distraction of all that abundance of hair and curves, accompanied by a disarming giggle.

Back in the kitchen Marco drank a glass of cold water and surreptitiously checked his reflection in the window. While he was distracted his father took Julie's drink out to her and Marco had to whisk plates off to table three, but he made sure he was the one to carry her *Spaghetti Bolognese* over. He had a marvellous glimpse of cleavage and lacy underwear as he placed her plate in front of her. His concentration had gone completely. To boldly go, where ... probably quite a few men have happily gone before, is what I would like to do, he thought, wielding the pepper grinder.

Oh no, the Star Trek misquote had conjured up a picture of Julie in a skin-tight uniform on the bridge of the Star Ship Enterprise. *Beam me up Scotty!*

He cleared his throat and asked if she wanted parmesan cheese.

'I dun' know. What do you think?'

'Well, my dear uncle would say that cheese on a *ragu,* on a meat sauce, is an abomination - but I say, you should do what you want.'

'That's what I always say ... I'll 'ave some then.'

Marco liked her voice. He liked the fact that her accent wasn't the perfect English that her boss spoke, which always reminded him of royalty and made him uncomfortable. Julie's voice always had a hint of a smile in it that matched her dimples. He decided that he would ask her out for a drink the following week, on his day off. Maybe he would take her a *rum baba* for her lunch on Monday. He was sure she would like it and he could tell her that the *baba* reminded him of her; plump, sweet and luscious.

12

199 Steps

Angelina Snow behind the wheel of a car was a force to be reckoned with. By the time they had negotiated the outskirts of Lincoln and were stopped at traffic lights that had been too emphatically red even for Angelina to ignore, Leo was exhausted. He had been surreptitiously braking and steering on his side of the car whilst trying to appear blasé, and he had had enough. He was sweating in spite of having removed his pullover. Fixing his gaze on the spire of Lincoln Cathedral showing above the roof tops, he cleared his dry throat.

'Madam, may I ask why we did not take the motorway? Surely it would have been faster and there would have been fewer obstacles for you to negotiate.'

'I never take the motorway when I drive to Whitby. This route is prettier and besides, the motorway traffic is always bad at this time of day,' she replied, shifting gears and speeding off again.

'Prettier maybe, safer, I doubt!' Leo said wryly and Angelina flashed him a sideways look.

'Why, Mr Marconi, I do believe you are scared,' she laughed.

'Absolutely terrified, madam,' he confessed. 'Not only are we on the wrong side of the road and have so far encountered at least a hundred roundabouts, where everyone hurls themselves around inside their lanes at incredible speed, we also appear to be trying to break the sound barrier.'

'Don't be silly, Leonardo. I thought it was Italians who were supposed to be the crazy drivers.'

Pleased that she had dropped the 'Mr Marconi', at least for now, Leo informed her that indeed most Italians were mad drivers, but he was not.

'I had my licence taken away earlier this year after I nearly died, but even before that my philosophy was that the best way to drive is *slowly*. I had a very reliable Fiat Panda and I found that as long as I kept to the speed limit I never had any problem with traffic at all. Everyone overtook me and then I had the road free for myself.'

Angelina decided to tease him a little. He had sounded so solemn when talking, and had such a deliciously cynical way of thinking that Angelina could not resist saying, 'Sometimes you remind me of Eeyore, you know.'

'My favourite character in the *Winnie–the–Pooh* books,' he declared with a smile.

Angelina decided to slow down a little to please him, and told him about how much fun she had had bringing up Hal.

'How he loved playing Pooh-sticks, racing our twig boats downstream by the little bridge. I should have known then that he would want to be a sailor one day. And how he used to laugh at the words Pooh, and wind, burp and fart.'

Leo sniggered and she shook her head in mock disgust.

'You see, all boys, no matter how old they are, find those things funny!'

Leo thought that in that moment, with her mother's instinct burning bright, she had never looked lovelier.

'How come you had to bring Hal up?' he wondered. Angelina sighed, serious again, and Leo regretted asking the question. However, after a moment, she looked at him briefly, weighing up how much she should say, and then shrugged as if loosening a weight on her shoulders. She began to speak slowly, selecting her words very carefully.

'My mother died when I was too young to remember much. Dad gave up his job in London and moved back to Bourne to spend more time with me, instead of commuting every day. I had Dad all to myself until he met Helen. I told my father how much I hated her — *and* him, for betraying my mother. I remember he sat down next to me and told me that he was sorry I felt like that, but I would get over it, and that one day I would understand that he would love my mother forever, just as he would love me. Of course I did not believe him.

'I look like him, you know, more than Hal does. Hal is golden like his mother. I am used to the way I look now, but growing up I hated being so tall and spiky, bones jutting out, especially my nose! Helen was lovely, so gentle, with soft hands, and she smelt wonderful, of the cakes she baked for me and a light perfume she knew my father liked.

'I stopped hating Dad quickly enough but was a little teenage brat with Helen. Then when I was seventeen she got pregnant. I was furious. I knew I would have to share Dad again and resented the baby enormously. As soon as Hal was born I changed my mind. I loved him from the start, and instead of feeling excluded Helen got me to help her and trusted me with him. One day I was watching her in the kitchen as she tried to spoon cereal into Hal's mouth and I asked her if she could forgive me. She looked at me for what seemed like ages and then said that she was not sure if I was ready to give up my hate yet, and that if I wanted to go on for a bit longer that was OK with her. I cried then and she held me, and it felt so good to be hugged.'

Angelina smiled wistfully at the bittersweet memory. She glanced at Leonardo to gauge his reaction. She never opened up like this, her private life was her own, not to be shared. His crumpled face and dark eyes moved into a small smile of encouragement and she knew that whatever she shared with him now would remain between the two of them.

'Those were the happiest days I can remember. Baby Halliwell Snow became my joy. He was the one who looked like the 'little angel', not me, and he had such a sunny temperament. When I left home to go to university I missed them all far more than I had expected, Hal in particular.

'Then, Dad and Helen were killed in a car crash.'

Angelina swallowed. Leo had so many questions he wanted to ask, but was afraid she would close up again if he made a sound. His heart ached for her, for all she had left unsaid, for the ugly girl she had felt herself to be, for her loneliness, and it seemed so unfair that life had taken away both mothers. No wonder she found it hard to show her feelings. She must be constantly aware of how easily love can be lost. When it became obvious Angelina was not going to say any more Leo asked, 'So, what did you do then?'

Angelina jumped as if she had been so far away in her memories that she had forgotten about him. Surprisingly, while she had been talking her driving had been slower and much less erratic, but now she put her foot down again and swerved past the car in front.

'I left university,' she said dully. 'There was no choice really, was there?' She straightened her shoulders and a small smile brightened her face.

'I never regretted it. The only time Hal and I argued was when I wanted to send him to our father's boarding-school and he declared that he would run away to sea if I did not want him. He lasted one term. He did everything he could to get expelled. He set off the fire alarms, climbed the chapel spire and refused to come down, ran away to walk in the fields instead of going to lessons. He was not academic anyway, and was so obviously miserable that I brought him home and sent him to the local school. I sold our big family home and put half the money away for Hal. He never touched it except to buy his boat. He lives like a tramp most of the time, says the only thing that is important is being free. With my half of the money I bought a smaller place for the two of us and started up the estate agency business. When Hal moved out and it was obvious he wasn't coming back to live with me I downsized to my present flat, which is much more convenient for work.'

Angelina glanced over at Leonardo and said rather defiantly, daring him to feel sorry for her, 'So, there you have it, my sad but uninteresting life.'

'You never married?' Leo asked, wondering even as the words left his mouth whether he was pushing too far, but to his relief she gave a dry laugh.

'No, no special men in my life after university. Not that I ever had to fight them off exactly, but that first year was fun. My problem is that I prefer men with brains — and they are very, very rare.'

Leo felt a faint stirring of hope. He was certainly not going to capture this splendid woman with his looks, but no matter how unpopular he had been in his life, no one had ever accused him of being unintelligent. The rest of the journey was spent in pleasant conversation as if one of those walls between them had been breached. Leo entertained her with stories about Rome and his life there — not mentioning his mother to avoid spoiling the atmosphere — and about sailing in the Mediterranean. He made her laugh several times and was feeling quite flushed with success by the time they reached Whitby.

It was just gone 4pm and the town was busy as they drove through. The streets were full of tourists eating ice-creams and stepping off the pavements in front of the car without looking, so that Angelina growled at them. Most people wore sweaters or fleeces over their summer clothes, and when they had parked in a large car park near the estuary and got out Leo understood why. The wind tugged at him with cold fingers and he was very pleased to put his pullover back on.

Angelina set off at a brisk pace toward the jetty where *Calypso* was moored and where Grace had said she would meet them. The wheels of her suitcase bounced over the kerbs and Leo hoped that the fastenings were secure. He followed at a more leisurely pace carrying her canvas holdall, his own bag swinging from his shoulder, reassuringly heavy with its supply of wine.

The water in the estuary was very low, but deep enough here for the boats to float. Leo spotted the elegant lines of Hal's Contest 40 immediately. She was a lovely old boat. Leo was of the opinion that modern boats were flimsy and clumsy in comparison. *Elisir* had been just such a boat, although a little bigger. He ran an expert eye over her rigging, noticing the little touches of a boat-proud owner. Dark blue sail and hatch covers looked tidy and fairly new, the chrome was recently polished and the woodwork gleamed. He was so taken up with his admiration that he failed to notice the woman sitting on the jetty at first.

'That must be Grace,' Angelina said, indicating the figure sitting hunched over, arms wrapped around her knees and head bent as if studying the water rippling below the planks. As she spoke, the girl looked up and raised an arm in greeting, then stood up waiting for them to join her. Simply dressed, in jeans, navy cardigan and a low-cut, white cotton top that contrasted with her velvet-brown skin, she looked fragile enough to blow away in a puff of wind. As he got closer, Leo could see that she had a beauty that came from somewhere other than her delicate features. There was a peaceful quality in her bearing, a way of holding herself that indicated composure, in spite of the uneasiness her dark eyes revealed. Her voice was no disappointment, being low and musical.

'Hello Angelina, thank you for coming,' she said, holding out her hand. Angelina introduced Leonardo and Grace took his hand too, smiling sweetly at him. Her hand was bare with no rings or nail-varnish, and felt surprisingly warm in his.

She handed Angelina a bunch of keys and nodded at the boat, saying, 'Please excuse me if I leave you immediately. The police have agreed to see me. I am going to try to convince them that I am not completely crazy.' She gave a self-deprecating smile and shook her head.

'You probably think I am nuts too, Angelina. The first contact you have with me is when I call you in a panic and talk about my visions.'

Angelina said nothing to contradict Grace, merely raised one eyebrow, looking quite intimidating, and Leo was glad he was not the one being subjected to such close examination. Angelina towered above the younger woman and her angular features were arranged in an expression of cool scrutiny, but Grace did not seem perturbed. She smiled gently again and continued speaking as if unaware of the frosty greeting.

'I am a bit less worried now than when I called you because I felt a connection with Hal earlier, and he didn't seem in such danger or pain any more. Yesterday, as I told you, I distinctly felt him falling and landing in great pain. I still feel that he is in a cold, dark, place but the pain has lessened, and I sense that there's someone with him.' While describing her sensations, Grace had closed her eyes and tipped her head to one side, as if looking inside at a picture only she could see.

'Clairsentience?' Leo asked, and Grace nodded.

'I beg your pardon?' Angelina asked in a frosty voice and Leo replied, 'It's from the French, *clair* meaning clear and *sentience* which means feeling, a type of extra-sensory perception, where a person understands something in a psychic way through an inner feeling.' He turned to Grace and asked, 'Does that come close?'

Grace smiled at him warmly.

'Close enough. Some people call it that. All I know is that my Grandma taught me from when I was a small child that there are extra dimensions for us to explore if we're not afraid to see. My gift has caused me a fair amount of trouble over the years, with those who fear the unknown, but it has also saved me from a lot of unpleasant experiences, and I have learnt not to ignore it.

'I've tried to call Hal,' she continued, 'but there is no reply so I think that either his phone is broken or there is no reception where he is.'

'I've tried too,' Angelina said, sounding friendly for the first time. 'If you weren't so worried, and if I hadn't seen Hal the other day and heard how keen he was to get back here to you, I would have said he had just decided to go off somewhere for a few days and forgotten to let you know.'

'No.' There was no doubt in Grace's voice. 'I don't know where he is, I can't see clearly but I know he needs help.' She handed over a scrap of paper with a list of local places where she had already searched and then, looking up at the sky where dark clouds were gathering, making it seem later that it was, she shrugged her shoulders.

'I don't suppose there is much more we can do today. I'll ring you after I've seen the police, OK?'

As Grace walked off quickly, Angelina looked at Leo with a bemused expression and said, 'I don't know whether to believe her and be really worried about Hal, or amused by her vivid imagination. She is extraordinary! I was almost convinced that she really can sense things that others can't. One thing I am certain of is that Hal would not have just gone off somewhere. He was intending to ask Grace to move in with him this weekend, I know that. I'm afraid I was very negative about it, but he did seem pretty determined. He even insisted on taking Helen's engagement ring away with him, although it did't seem to occur to him that Grace might read more into that than he intended.'

'Could he have got cold feet?' Leo asked. Angelina smiled and shook her head.

'No, he wasn't ready to make the big step of a formal relationship, I admit, but I know my Hal, and I've never seen him so obviously in love and happy.

'I should have known he wouldn't fall for anyone remotely normal,' she added dryly as she hauled herself aboard.

Leo handed the luggage up to her, then swung on board himself. He smiled in ecstasy as the pretty vessel dipped and tugged at her moorings. He felt at home immediately and stared longingly towards the mouth of the estuary and the beckoning silver of the open sea beyond.

'Come on, Captain Ahab,' Angelina said sarcastically. 'Let's get this stuff stowed and we can start looking for Hal.' She wrestled with the key and finally got the hatch open, then they reversed positions, Leo taking the luggage from her as she lowered it down the stairs.

What a lovely boat. Leo ran his fingers appreciatively over the honeyed wood and nodded approvingly at the sight of the neat galley to starboard, flanked by a comfortable semi-circular settee covered in pretty yellow fabric. Angelina descending the steep stairs backwards was a rather pleasant sight too. Leo unashamedly enjoyed watching the way the black linen moulded to her backside, then turned away quickly before she could catch him looking. There was another enchanting moment when she squeezed past him in the narrow galley and opened the door to the front cabin.

The twin V-berths were both made up with crisp white sheets folded back over multi-coloured striped quilts.

'Grace must have made up the beds for us — Hal would never have been so tidy. Last time I came to visit I had to clear away his rubbish before I could get at my bunk.'

'She made up both of them,' Leo observed.

'So she did. Maybe she really *is* clairvoyant or clair-whatever,' Angelina said, casting a doubtful glance at the second bed.

Leo understood what she was thinking and immediately offered to sleep on the couch in the galley, but she raised an eyebrow at him and reminded him that they were both adults and her biggest worry was where she was going to put her clothes. Leo indicated the size of his bag to demonstrate that he would not be using up precious storage space, then opened a wardrobe door just outside the cabin. *Marvellous storage in this boat, too.* If it wasn't for the fact that Hal had his foul weather gear stored there Angelina would have been able to hang everything up. He pointed out some spacious cubby-holes alongside each bunk, but she looked at him blankly. The woman was just not at home on a boat. There were also four nice-sized drawers below the bunks, and Grace had obviously been at work there too, since he noticed that two of them were empty. Leo nobly offered Angelina all the space there was.

'I can leave my stuff in my bag,' he told her and then, seeing that this lack of space was a rather large hurdle for her to overcome, backed out and let her do the best she could while he bustled around in the galley and prepared to make some coffee. He was just about to investigate where the gas was located to turn it on, when Angelina reappeared with a half-full suitcase and a look of desperation. This was partly because, when she came to unpack, she had been surprised by what she found in the case. She was sure she had packed some comfortable old brushed-cotton pyjamas and had, instead, been astonished to find, hidden under the grey sweater, a pair of chocolate-brown pyjamas with a pale blue trim, and a matching dressing gown; and, even more astonishing, a totally impractical ivory silk nightdress with shoe string straps that criss-crossed at the back to make sure you did not lose it, since the back plunged to within an inch of the base of the spine. How had *those* got in there? Angelina had absolutely no memory of packing them. She had forgotten the 'night things' she had stuffed in at the last minute after Mr Marconi's unscheduled arrival.

'Let's go out for a drink,' she said firmly. 'I can think better on dry land.' If he was not mistaken, she was looking a bit green. It must be the soft motion of the boat at its moorings, which he had been enjoying so much. They locked up, put Angelina's case back in her car boot and walked along the banks of the estuary into Whitby. They crossed the bridge into the old part of town because Angelina had fixed on the idea of climbing up to the ruined Benedictine Abbey. She said that whenever Hal needed to think about serious things he would always try to be high up.

'When he was tiny I used to find him hiding on the top shelf of the airing cupboard, curled up around the cat. The reason he gave when he climbed up the chapel spire at school was that he had needed to think somewhere where he could not be disturbed,' she remembered with a wry grimace.

'I even sent him on a rock-climbing course when he was fifteen in the hope that if he had the skill he wouldn't risk getting hurt so much,' she said, and pushed her hair away from her face as the worry swept back over her.

'You were a good mother,' Leo said gently, and she smiled down at him and rested her hand lightly on his sleeve.

'I certainly tried to be,' she replied, and strode off again through the narrow lanes packed with tourists, ignoring the quaint old shops and the opulent displays of local jet glinting in jewellers' windows.

Angelina showed no sign of slowing her pace, and he thought she had forgotten all about the idea of a drink. She was worried again and her forehead was creased into a frown. He had seen her alternating all day between worry and frustration, uncertain if there was any real problem but caring too much to ignore the possibility.

Leo himself was quite unperturbed. Hal had seemed to be a very capable man and Leo had been surprised by how much he had liked him at first meeting. Leo was suspicious by nature and gave his friendship very unwillingly, but there had been something very beautiful about Angelina's brother. Whether it was his shining good looks, the innocent and frank blue-eyed gaze or his open manner, Leo couldn't say. However, he had found that the time he had spent in Hal's company had lifted his spirits. He thought that more than likely Hal had simply gone somewhere to contemplate the huge step he was thinking of making, and it seemed to be his way to contemplate events in remote places. Then again, any number of minor mishaps could have happened: the car might have broken down when he was in an area with no phone reception, or he could have gone to a friend's house, got thoroughly drunk and completely forgotten about letting anyone know. He would probably be flabbergasted when he found out what a fuss he had caused. No, Leo was not worried at all — but he was very grateful to Hal for providing him with this marvellous opportunity of getting closer to Angelina.

The object of his desire walked past a delightful looking pub, with colourful hanging baskets and chalk boards offering local ales, without giving it a glance. She turned to the right and began to walk up some shallow steps. Leo stopped. He had seen the sign on the wall that informed him that there would be 199 of those steps to climb — and the pub looked so welcoming.

'Maybe we could have that drink you mentioned before we climb those steps?'

Angelina turned round and looked at Leonardo's hopeful expression as he gestured to the Duke of York, which *did* look quite nice — and she *was* very thirsty, now that she had stopped to think about it, so she nodded and allowed him to usher her into the warm, beer-scented dimness inside. The pub was busy but Leo, with the instinct of a dedicated drinker, made his way quickly to the bar and pointed out a table for two by the French windows, overlooking the estuary. She asked for a tonic water and sat down heavily. She had no energy left, she realised, and called out to ask Leo to get some crisps too. She would feel better if she ate something. Leonardo was already being served. She listened to him asking for a tonic water and thought once more what a lovely voice he had, deep and resonant. She was suddenly very glad that he was with her.

***

'Two tonic waters, please,' Leo said. He had decided that he needed a clear head if he was going to keep up with Angelina on the steps later. Then he took a step back in astonishment as Drowned Leo sidled up to him, plonked himself on a bar stool and said, 'Add a large gin to mine!'

Not again, thought Leo. He was seriously worried about his sanity if his doppelganger could appear when he was sober. He became aware that he was staring at an empty bar-stool and that the barman had asked him a question.

'Sorry?' he said.

'Ice and lemon in those?' asked the barman.

'Oh, why not, let's push the boat out.' Leo couldn't resist the sarcasm and earned himself a caustic glance from Angelina. 'And a packet of salted crisps.'

Deliberately ignoring Drowned Leo as he skirted around his bar stool, Leonardo carried the drinks and crisps over to the table and plonked himself down on the pink velvet chair. He risked a quick glance toward the bar, but the apparition had, thankfully, disappeared. Leo made a mental note to see a doctor on his return, to discuss his disturbing hallucinations. Taking a sip of the tonic water he made a face and was pleased to see

Angelina smile. The ripples in the estuary glinted silver and seagulls swooped around, keening impatiently as they waited for the fishing fleet. It would have been a very pleasant place to spend an evening; first a few drinks while watching the tide slowly turn, then ordering something from the menu he could see on a board by the bar. However, after allowing a brief smile to ease her frown, Angelina had downed her tonic water in several large and unladylike gulps and was ready to go. Leo drank his a little more slowly, but he understood that she could not sit still and enjoy the moment when her thoughts were on Hal.

Outside, the 199 steps awaited. There were a lot of them. 199 to be exact. Leo did not count them but he believed the signs that proudly boasted the fact. What he could vouch for was that they were awkward. They were shallow and wide — he could not get a good rhythm going and had to keep changing his leading foot. Angelina had no such problem with her long legs, but even she was out of puff by the time they reached the top. The steps ended in St Mary's sprawling old graveyard. Bits of the abbey's ruined walls could be seen at the top of the slope, and groups of tourists meandered between the wonky, moss-covered graves while children jigged up and down trying to get the attention of two shaggy and highly indifferent ponies in the field by the wall.

Leo glanced behind him at Whitby sprawled out below with the river cutting it in two. In the harbour the boats seemed tiny, their masts swaying as the river played with them. A stout old couple walked in front of them and Leo heard the wife say, 'I can't see the whale bones from here, can you Arthur?'

'Whale bones?' Leo asked Angelina, wondering if the climb had affected his hearing.

'Whitby used to have a whaling fleet, and on the west cliff over there is an arch made from whale bones at the top of a flight of steps leading down into the town. The original ones are in a museum now but—' Angelina broke off suddenly. She looked around her at the stark shapes of the Abbey ruins in the twilight and felt tears pricking her eyes.

'What am I *doing* here? If Hal were here he would have been found by now. This is pointless.' She sounded so despondent that Leo felt he had to do something to help, but he had no idea what. Still, if in doubt, never let others know, that was one of his mottoes.

'There is nothing else we can do tonight, so we will go and have something to eat, get a good night's sleep, and in the morning we will find Hal,' he said decisively. To his surprise Angelina nodded agreement, and she did not shrug off the solicitous hand he placed in the small of her back as they began the long descent back into town.

13

The Light in the Tunnel

In the dim glow from his flashlight, stumbling over the landslide he had caused, Hal made his way towards the old man's voice as it drifted away, as if blown by an unseen air current. When he reached the darker patch he had assumed to be a tunnel or second cave he hesitated, reluctant to move deeper into this underground world, even though he was convinced that there was no way out of the cave he had fallen into unless someone found him and sent down a rope. Since no one knew where he was, and it was doubtful that the hole he had fallen through would be visible from the path he had walked along the previous day, this seemed a very unlikely scenario.

'Light thyself the torch on the wall and tread warily, Halliwell,' the voice whispered from the darkness ahead. Hal shone his flashlight around the entrance to the tunnel and saw a niche on the right with an ancient torch made of a stout stick with some kind of fabric wrapped around the top. Feeling ridiculously like Indiana Jones, he rummaged around in his rucksack for his lighter and put the flame to the end of the torch. To his surprise it caught fire easily, and the brighter light it sent flickering around the tunnel was instantly comforting. Turning off his small flashlight he wondered how long the smouldering torch would last.

As if reading his mind, a whisper, unnervingly close to his ear said, 'It should give thee light for almost two shadows on the dial. However, so much time has passed since I made it that I cannot tell exactly how long it will burn.' The soft voice moved away along the tunnel, quickly becoming so faint that Hal almost missed the next words, but thought he had understood that there would be other torches along the way to guide him. Hal took a hesitant step into the tunnel, slightly reassured by the lively glow that illuminated the rock walls well enough for him to make out nearby cracks and striations and the occasional runnel of water that seeped through the rock. The underground world smelt of damp stone and musty air. Hal straightened his shoulders and quickened his pace, not wanting to discover how claustrophobic the tunnel would feel without his torch for company or the sound of the strange old man's voice.

Two shadows on the dial? Maybe that meant two hours. But who *was* the old man, where the heck was he, and why did he speak in that strange way? Hal rubbed his sore head, wondering just how much damage his fall had caused. He could hear the voice again, echoing faintly, as if the unseen man was talking to himself. No matter how hard Hal strained his eyes, he could not catch a glimpse of his invisible companion, not even a light or shadow. He could not hear everything that was said but it sounded like snippets of a story.

At the heart is the holy well, that is the goal, the reward of the quest .... called me healer ....

I did no harm that night but could not heal the great man's son, no one could .... pain of loss turned his heart to stone .... and closed my way forever .... buried ..... Now the young knight will take up my cause ... free my soul.

The hairs rising on his arms at the ghostly unreality of it all, as if he were inside a compelling nightmare, Hal stumbled on. He was either alone in a maze of windypit tunnels and hearing hallucinatory voices, or in the company of a madman raving of knights and quests and holy wells. Holy well: the meaning of his own name. Hal concluded that he must indeed be suffering from concussion.

The tunnel that had started high and wide now began to lower and close in on Hal, so that he had to stoop. He was tired now. Since he never wore a watch, with his phone out of use he had no way of knowing the time, which made everything even more unreal. Was it day or night? His head hurt, and he was bruised and sore from the fall and the time spent buried under the landslide. The old man, if he were not merely a creature of the imagination, was always just around a corner or too far ahead to see. Hal contemplated turning back. Who knew where this tunnel might lead to? Touching the pouch in his pocket, Hal thought of Grace's face. Those adorable freckles on coffee-coloured skin, her warm brown eyes smiling at him, and her lips curving gently as she leant in to anticipate his kiss.

'Nay, do not stray in thy mind.' Suddenly the old man's voice spoke harshly, seemingly from just behind him, and Hal jerked to a halt.

'Give thine attention to the path. Stay close to the wall,' the voice said — but when Hal swung his torch to look behind him the tunnel was empty. He began to edge closer to the tunnel wall, then froze as a cold energy seized his shoulder and a force invaded his mind. 'NO, to the left side, keep thee close to the left, Halliwell.'

Hal shuddered, then moved slowly forward, his left shoulder scraping the low tunnel wall until a few yards further on his torch revealed a gaping hole that was almost as wide as the passage, and so deep that he could not see the bottom. He steeled himself to inch his way along the small ledge. His feet crunched in dirt and gravel rather than smooth rock, presumably the result of the cave-in that had created the hole. It added to his feeling of vulnerability, especially when the small stones he dislodged fell silently, giving the impression that the hole was bottomless.

He found himself sweating suddenly as fear gripped him, and once on the far side of the hole, he slid down the damp rock to ease the trembling in his legs. He felt quite light-headed with terror and exhaustion, and at the same time exhilarated as adrenalin surged though his body.

Up ahead, the old man began to mumble again, and as the voice drifted further away Hal pushed himself to his feet and wearily followed. Madman, ghost or imagination, the voice had saved his bacon, Hal thought, hurrying to catch up. From now on, he vowed, he would stick closer and pay attention to whatever he heard.

14

Seagull Luck

Grace drove slowly along the coastal road as she tried to get used to the Land Rover she had borrowed. Charlie from the boatyard had not hesitated when she had asked if she could borrow it, just nodded and tossed the keys at her, saying casually, 'You'll find it yonder, lass. You can bring it back tomorrow. That there policeman is neither use nor ornament.' Then he had turned back to the planks he was sanding. When she had tried to thank him he had scowled at her and sent her off with a brusque but kindly, 'Stop faffing around and go find the lad, will you!'

The Land Rover was much bigger than her own car and she was scared of misjudging the width. How she missed her little Volkswagen Beetle — and if Charlie had heard her crunch the gears as she came round that last bend, she imagined that he would have regretted his generosity. She hoped that she could get it back to him without a scratch.

Her meeting with the police had been as frustrating as she had feared. The officer she had spoken to had listened quite politely, nodded sagely when she had described her 'feelings' and done quite a good job (but not quite good enough) of masking his opinion that she was a crackpot. He had promised to tell his men to keep an eye out for Hal and let her know if he was sighted. If he was not home in a few days she should let him know and they would step up the search.

After that, she had gone back to the boat to see if Angelina and Leonardo were OK, but found it empty. Then she had seen Charlie in the workshop and decided to try another tack. If she could borrow a car, she could drive along the coast and see if she could feel Hal's presence anywhere. Maybe if she got closer to him her sensations would be stronger.

Charlie, a burly, taciturn Yorkshire man with wild grey curls, had put down his tools and listened quietly to her story. Unlike the police officer, with his steady gaze he had been non-judgemental and comforting. Charlie had been a fisherman until an accident left him with a crippled right foot. After that he had bought a share in the old boatyard so that he could still be close to the sea. When his partner had died a few years later, Charlie had taken over the whole business. He and Hal had been friends since Hal had first arrived in Whitby. Charlie had given him some part-time work in the boatyard and taken him under his wing. Having no children of his own, Grace thought that the older man saw in Hal a kind of surrogate son, and recently Hal had been considering the proposition that Charlie had put to him of becoming a partner in the yard and working with him to expand the business and build a larger version of the sturdy Whitby Coble fishing boats.

Grace was relieved to see that her story had not flummoxed Charlie at all, perhaps because he possessed the fisherman's innately superstitious nature, or maybe he too thought that Hal would not have disappeared without letting anyone know. Whatever the reason, Grace was very grateful to him.

First she had driven north along the coast to some of the places she and Hal loved. Pretty, Sandsend Bay was idyllic in the early evening sun. Some families remained on the beach, with children squealing as they ran away from the gentle waves, throwing wet sand over their weary parents, and indefatigably filling buckets for their wonky sandcastles. She drove through the car park and out again when she saw that her Volkswagen was not there. Today the car park was clean, unlike other times when she and Hal had parked there to watch the sea when it was rough and pounding the beach, waves washing into the car park and leaving it strewn with seaweed.

She drove on as far as Staithes, where they loved to walk along the footpath that skirted the village, looking down on the rooftops and the spectacular views of the cliffs beyond, and then have a drink in the pub by the harbour. However, her car was not there either, and by this time Grace felt that she was moving further away from Hal. She should head back, she decided.

She felt pulled southwards, probably because she knew Hal would have driven that way coming back from Angelina's house. She had not sensed his energy for a while now, and she tried to take comfort from that. She was so very tired. The previous night, she had needed company and had stayed with her grandma instead of going upstairs to her own flat. Clair understood Grace like no one else, and Grace always found her sympathy and steady strength very comforting. Tucked up in Grandma Clair's bed, listening to her gentle snoring, Grace had probed the darkness for hours, trying in vain to recreate that flash of connection. During the day there had been a couple of occasions when she had sensed his presence at the edge of her conscious mind, and had been reassured when the original flash of pain and fear had not been repeated.

She turned the car left toward Robin Hood Bay and began the descent, taking extra care on the bends and keeping an eye out for a glimpse of the Beetle parked along the side streets. She reached the car park in front of the Victoria Hotel, a rather attractive building and probably a lovely hotel to stay in, but memorable for her because of one thirty minute wait for Hal's bacon sandwich, during which his stomach had demonstrated its capacity to make rumbles of orchestral proportions. When the sandwich finally arrived, Hal had devoured it in a few huge bites in spite of the bacon being burnt to a crisp. After that they had always walked down into the village to eat, following the seawall walk, sometimes pausing to sit a while on one of the benches that faced the sea and marvel at its many-faceted beauty. Hal loved the days when storms buffeted the coast and spray dampened their skin as they walked. He always said how glad he was not to be at sea in *Calypso* on a day like that and to be headed for a nice cosy pub instead.

She remembered one morning when they had been admiring the seagulls that battled the high winds, and one of them had decided to investigate them too. It had swooped low and deposited a huge poop on Hal's shoulder. Oh, the look of indignation on his face! He had been quite cross until she had managed to wipe most of it off with a tissue and — between wheezes of laughter — reassure him that it was very lucky to receive such a gift.

Grace preferred the days when the tide was out, leaving fingers of kelp-strewn sand, dotted with gulls and cormorants, shimmering wetly whenever the sun peeked through the glowering clouds. How wonderful it would be to know that Hal was waiting for her at the Smugglers' Nest. They would sit, holding hands under the table, enjoying the romantic candlelit ambience. They would laugh at her fears for him and eat garlic bread together while he decided how big a steak he could manage and she chose something special from the vegetarian menu. However, there was no sign of her car here either, and with a sinking heart Grace pulled over to the side of the road and closed her eyes against the tears that suddenly prickled hotly there. She leant over the wheel, feeling the cool centre on her forehead. A sudden flood of emotion raised goose-pimples over her skin and her scalp felt hyper-sensitive.

Hal was standing on the threshold of a deep, dark pit. He was lit by some kind of flickering light, from a flame or fire of some sort. His face was determined but white beneath streaks of dirt. She felt her heart beat faster, taking on the rhythm of Hal's as he inched his way along a narrow shelf, feet just inches away from the chasm.

A loud banging brought her back to the present, and she sat up jerkily and wound down her window to hear a worried looking, red-faced man ask her if she was all right.

'I live nearby. Can I offer you a cup of tea maybe, or should I call a doctor?'

'No, I'm sorry to worry you. I feel fine, just a bit tired.' Grace summoned up a smile from somewhere and stuck it on her face to reassure him. She drove off before he could insist, and made it to the top of the hill before she pulled over and parked properly, wondering which way to go now. This time when she closed her eyes she willed herself to get a sense of where Hal was, even just the general direction would do. The vision had gone completely but she could feel him, a slight echo within her heartbeat, and she nodded slightly, straightened her shoulders and headed toward Pickering. It was growing dark by now. The beautiful moorland with its heather and fern was indistinct in the dusk. She drove through Pickering and on toward Thirsk. As the car descended from Sutton Bank she shivered. She was tired and it was now completely dark. There was nothing more she could do today, and at least she was now sure that Hal was alive— in danger but alive — and that was all that mattered. She would find a place to stay overnight in Thirsk, ring Grandma Clair and then Angelina to tell them where she had looked, and then start again in the morning.

As she reached the outskirts of Thirsk she felt a deep ache in the pit of her stomach. She had gone too far. She had passed him by somehow, but he was closer than before, and in the morning she *would* find him. She concentrated on the traffic around the busy old town, but at the same time kept an eye out for guest houses along the way. Turning towards the James Herriot Museum, her attention was caught by a cottage advertising itself as a guest house, with a red front door surrounded by hanging baskets. She had an immediate sensation of warmth, friendliness and ... dogs. Trusting her instinct, she parked the car and approached the guest house. Sure enough, she was greeted by loud barking, and when the door opened, several small wet noses at different heights pushed out before the short, rotund owner could extend her own plump hand.

'Welcome, my dear,' the lady said, pushing the dogs away.

'Kitchen!' she ordered sharply, and three of the dogs trotted obediently toward the back of the house. The other, a Golden Labrador as plump as its owner, plonked itself on its rump instead and looked up at its mistress indignantly. Grace crouched down and stroked the soft ears. She was rewarded with a wet slurp across her cheek and laughed, despite her anxious mood.

'You'll be wanting a room for just the night then?' asked the lady, and Grace nodded, standing up reluctantly. The unconditional affection of dogs was so comforting. Maybe she and Hal would get one someday. There was nothing better, to her mind, than children and dogs growing up together.

The lady introduced herself as Mrs Wolstenholme, 'but that's such a long name to remember dear, just call me Mrs Wuz — that is what I call myself when I talk to myself, isn't it Jess?' she chattered on, talking indiscriminately to both Grace and the dog as she bustled along the hallway. Jess pricked up her ears at the sound of her name and padded along at Grace's heels, pressing her bulk against her legs once she had stopped until Grace reached down to fondle her ears again.

'Have you eaten, or shall I make you something'? Mrs Wuz asked with a critical glance at Grace's slim shape. Grace declined politely, saying she was not hungry, and closed the door on both inquisitive gazes as quickly as she could without being rude. She felt alarmingly close to tears, overwhelmed by the sincere welcome she had just received after a day spent in lonely contemplation of her fears. Mrs Wuz was a woman who liked to get her own way, however, and a short while later she knocked at Grace's door and handed her a tray laden with cheese sandwiches, buttered scones and a pot of tea.

'Just eat what you fancy and leave the rest. The dogs are always happy to eat leftovers!' she said, laid a kindly hand on Grace's arm for a second and then turned away, clicking her tongue to call Jess, who showed signs of wanting to stay and guard the food.

Hours later, Grace snuggled into the fresh cotton sheets and tried to sleep. She had been tossing and turning for ages. Her mind was full of fear and dramatic scenarios that had nothing to do with visions of Hal, but were instead just her imagination doing its worst. Grace was cross with herself. She should be able to still these images and calm herself, but her mind was on its hamster wheel and refused to get off. The last curling, half-eaten sandwich sat on the dressing table. The rest of them, and the delicious scones, lay heavily in her stomach.

The room felt somewhat over-heated, so Grace got up and opened the window, gratefully drawing in deep breaths of cool night air. Then she crossed the landing to the bathroom and splashed cold water on her face and wrists. Her face in the mirror looked haggard, with dark smudges beneath her eyes, and her lips were dry from being bitten unconsciously all day. How different she would have looked if Hal had not mysteriously vanished and things had gone according to plan: an intimate dinner on *Calypso* and then a night together between their own sheets. She shrugged, rummaged in her handbag for her lip salve, then turned off the light and climbed back into bed.

This time she lay on her back, laid the fingers of her right hand over the gold cross above her breast and stretched out, beginning to breathe slowly and deliberately, using her meditation technique to calm her mind. Slowly the rumble of traffic on the street outside blended with the thud of her heartbeat and the slow flow of blood though her. It was working. Her mind was stilling with each deep breath. Rumi's words slid through her mind — *listen to the sound of the waves within you* — and she smiled. It was amazing how often the words of the thirteenth century Sufi poet and mystic could sum up what she felt.

Opening her mind and heart to the universe she concentrated on the sound of those inner waves until she could almost hear the sea breathing, and from behind her closed lids watch gentle snow falling. In those precious moments just before sleep, she added Hal's heartbeat to hers and the universe seemed her close and beloved friend and ally as they breathed easily together.

15

English Fish and Chips

After all the excitement of the day, 199 steps up and as many going down, Leonardo was very hungry. On his way back down the steps he had remembered a scene from Bram Stoker's *Dracula*, in which the ghastly Count himself set foot, or maybe it would be more correct to say paw, on English soil in the form of a huge dog. The ship carrying Dracula had crashed on the cliffs of Whitby, and the dog had bounded up the steep cliff towards the churchyard. This rather grisly thought had pleased Leo and filled him with admiration for a creature able to bound up that steep incline, but he thought it better not to share it with Angelina, who needed cheering up, not scaring, tonight.

Ghastly stuff, English fish and chips, Leo thought. Instead of freshly grilled fish with a hint of garlic and rosemary, here everything was thickly coated with batter. They had examined the menus of several restaurants before settling on this one, and Angelina had been getting irritated by his quest to find a good restaurant. He had described *La Paranza* to her, a little trattoria in Anzio where the local catch was served in a series of delicious dishes. Antipasti of small fish, lightly fried and served whole, that burnt your fingers as you picked them up; a mountain of spaghetti glistening with olive oil and dotted with clams and red chillies, followed by a whole grilled *orata,* all served with a huge carafe of chilled white wine. Angelina had laughed and told him to give up and settle for the English equivalent. So now he was crunching through the batter that surrounded a piece of cod. The local beer was good, though. He had quickly finished a pint but had restrained himself from ordering another because Angelina was nursing her half-pint and looking anxious again. Grace had just phoned to say she was in Thirsk and would stay the night. Angelina needed a distraction.

'I was married once,' he disclosed, and was gratified to see the worry lines on her face change to an expression of curiosity.

'Yes, but luckily for me she found someone else, and I was happy to let him keep her. I never had much luck with women. I moved back in with my dear old mother! She died last year, at the ripe old age of 96. I thought she never would. I came home each day worried that I would find she had decided to leave all her worldly goods to the church, just to spite me. She had an incredible knack for making the men in her life miserable. She sent my father to an early grave with her constant nagging and complaining, and once he was gone she kindly treated me to years of the same.'

Leonardo told his story with such dry humour that Angelina could not help laughing, which, she suspected, was what he had been hoping for. Once more, she was glad of his company. One day it would be nice to go to that small restaurant in Anzio he had described, she mused, and then felt herself blush. If Leonardo knew she had been imagining being in Italy with him ... heavens, what was wrong with her? She got up abruptly and stomped to the bar, where she paid the bill and ignored Leonardo as he tried to pay too. Feeling reassured now that she had asserted herself, she made him march to keep up with her as they headed back to the boat.

The jetty was in darkness and the water lapped oily-black against *Calypso's* hull. She let Leonardo open up and descend the steps first. He had no trouble locating the main switch, and once the lights were on, the boat looked more welcoming. The prow cabin with its two narrow beds that joined in a V was suddenly all too evident. *Good Lord, our feet will touch*, Angelina thought, and then, glancing at Leonardo, was reassured by his stature. His feet would not reach so far. He cleared his throat and turned to the stairs again, mumbling something about having a last cigarette.

***

The awkward moment had passed. Angelina was inside the head and Leo could hear her making abundant use of the water. He smiled in the dark, enjoying the warm glow from his cigarette as he drew on it. He was imagining Angelina on board with him as they sailed the warm Mediterranean Sea. No tides to worry about, maybe a night crossing between the Tyrrhenian Islands with the salty breeze still fairly warm, and stars huge without the shore lights to dim them. However, he mused, hearing a muffled yelp as Angelina knocked herself against something below, the woman was really not cut out for boat life — that much was obvious. Then again, Leo realised with a jolt, he no longer had a boat waiting for him in Rome. He missed *Elisir* enormously and had been furious when he had been obliged to sell her, but the doctor had been quite clear. He would always be at risk from high blood pressure without his medication, and sailing alone was not to be recommended. Being on board this lovely little ketch now was wonderful, but he was glad that he was not alone. He felt like a different person tonight and sensed that he was close to a new life that would be very good indeed.

There was a loud bang now and Angelina swore to herself, the actual words muffled but the meaning clear. Leo stifled a laugh. There were definite advantages to being short when on a boat. He fitted neatly under all doorways and rarely bumped himself on anything. His heart felt surprisingly light and full. He waited until he heard the door to the head open, then tossed his cigarette stub into the water and went below deck.

Leo was impressed by the head. Hal had fitted a holding tank to collect waste matter when in port. He had kept the very sensible old-fashioned style toilet with a sturdy pump mechanism, instead of one of these modern flush systems that tended to break down and leave you with a highly unpleasant mess when sailing. He particularly liked the way the sink was contained within a handy drawer above the toilet, which could be stowed within the wall when not being used. Such an inventive use of space. He had the feeling that Angelina would have a different opinion of the room. He could smell her perfume lingering in the air and there was a large wash-bag hanging on the handle of the cupboard over the sink, the cupboard itself being full of Hal's gear and various medical supplies. At the thought of her expression as she tried to find space for her things, Leo chuckled to himself, then swiftly changed into the pyjamas which he had thought to hang up over the shower-head earlier, and went to join her.

***

As Leonardo vaulted easily up onto his bunk, looking rather sweet in his paisley pyjamas, Angelina ruefully rubbed the new bruise on her shin that the same manoeuvre had given her. He rustled around under the covers getting comfortable for a while, and then cleared his throat — but said nothing. They lay there in the dark, each stiffly aware of the other.

'Maybe I should warn you that I snore,' Leonardo told her. 'If you like, I can go and sleep in the dinette?'

'I am sure that will not be necessary,' she reassured him. 'Goodnight, Leonardo.'

'Good night, Angelina.'

Angelina soon discovered that Leonardo had not been exaggerating. Within three minutes he had started to snore. She knew that this was going to be a terribly long night, and wondered if she should move to Hal's cabin — but that would involve finding keys, going outside, unlocking the rear cabin, and then goodness knows what state that would be in.

She tried making small clicking, hissing sounds. No luck. She even tried calling out his name, but the snores reverberated rhythmically on without the slightest pause. In desperation Angelina took her pillow and whacked him with it. This time Leonardo muttered, 'Sorry, was I snoring?' and rolled over. She tucked the pillow back under her head and relaxed into it. Seconds later the sawing noise started up again, but thankfully by that time Angelina was asleep too, as the exhausting day finally caught up with her.

16

Petrified Remains

Hal had no idea how long he had been following the uncanny voice through the windypit tunnels. He had long since lost his sense of orientation. He had bashed his head on a low rock formation a while back and opened up the wound on his forehead again. He wiped sticky blood from his cheek with his sleeve, relieved that the flow seemed to be slowing. The tunnel roof was very low here, and he was shaking with the effort of moving crouched over with knees bent for so long. If they did not stop soon, so that he could rest, he knew that he would probably pass out.

He had lit new torches twice in the labyrinth of passages, but this last one had burnt very low. He did not want to have to use his flashlight because the torch's flickering glow was not only brighter but also comforting, with the warmth of fire and the smoky scent that made him cough but was convincingly real. Nothing else was. His own body felt unfamiliar, slow and clumsy from pain and the loss of blood. He was even unsure whether the voice he was following really existed or if it was a kind of hallucination brought on by stress and concussion.

The most disturbing thing was that he was not hungry either. He had made himself stop occasionally and sip from his water bottle, but the chocolate and energy bars remained untouched — and since the only time he had ever lost his appetite before had been when he was running a fever, Hal knew from this that he was not at all well.

'Almost there, lad. It is a place where thee can rest a while. Methinks thou hast need of it now.'

'Good!' Hal replied shortly.

As the day had drawn on, he had become almost accustomed to the eerie voice that first muttered far ahead of him and then chilled his neck as it breathed near his ear. If he had believed in ghosts, he would have been convinced that he was being led through this underworld by a very courteous yet crazy spectre. Whatever it was, he would never have avoided falling into the deep pit or have known which passageway to choose as he moved deeper into the tunnels without it. He just hoped he would not end up in the company of Hades! Before he could bring to mind the various legends associated with the wily god of the unseen realm, there was a sudden change in the air that brought his incoherent thoughts back to his immediate surroundings.

The air smelt fresher here, and there was a pleasant sound of water dribbling over rocks nearby. Hal's torch dimly illuminated a large cavern with irregular walls, its ceiling and floor studded with creamy-white deformations. Moon-milk, he remembered, thinking how surprised his geography teacher would have been to know that some of his lessons had sunk in. He stepped further into the cave, casting his light around to see where the sound of water was coming from. He was grateful that he would be able to refill his water bottle and have a long drink without rationing it. He was very aware that his mind was unclear and wandering. Tired and confused, he nevertheless found himself fascinated by the strange stubby stalactites above.

'Stalactites hold on tight,' he muttered, feeling an absurd impulse to giggle. The voice was ominously quiet. Had he lost the old man, somehow? Hal raised his torch and, moved forward, tripping over the uneven deposits on the cave floor. Then he saw the source of the water. On his right, about a foot from the cave wall, there was a kind of natural stone basin where water bubbled up, as if from an underground spring.

'The holy well,' intoned the voice loudly. Maybe it was the acoustics of the cave that made the voice resonate louder than before, because Hal could still not see any sign of the man. Holy water or not, Hal was thirsty. He swiftly crossed over to the well, feeling his senses sharpening at the thought of delicious cool water. He plunged his hand into the hollow rock, scooped up a handful of water, and was just lowering his head to it when something caught his eye and he froze.

Shakily raising his torch, Hal stared in horror at the skeleton propped against the wall a few feet away. It had been there so long that small deposits of moon-milk grew from it in cancerous lumps, so that it seemed like a petrified part of the wall. He noted with disgust the remnants of leather sandals beneath the delicate bones of the toes. The body must have been there for centuries, he realised, letting out a shaky breath and wiping his face with the icy water in an effort to calm his pounding heart. He now noticed that there was a small metal cup on a ledge by the well, within reach of the skeleton. He would not have died of thirst, then. Hal knew who this must be even before the voice spoke, a hoarse whisper now, filled with regret.

'Nay, Halliwell, no need for thy sorrow. I have been here too long for thee to be aggrieved for me.'

'How long?' Hal's voice was hoarse with emotion.

'How long?' the voice repeated. Now Hal understood the unearthly quality to the speech he had been hearing; whispering like air, burbling like water, echoing hollowly through the tunnels, intangible and insubstantial. 'A good question, lad. Centuries, seconds? Time enough to face every soul that I harmed unintentionally in my life and to make amends. I could not fell my shadow in the dark and so became that very shadow.... I finally learnt to love even that.'

'Christ!' Hal swore unsteadily and sank down, leaning back on the cold rock next to the skeleton. He shook his head in disbelief. How could this be happening to him? His original belief that he was suffering from concussion seemed very fragile with the cold bones of the dead man sprawled beside him.

'It's like something from the tales of King Arthur,' he muttered beneath his breath. Surprisingly, the old man laughed at that, the sound echoing eerily around the cavern.

'Nay, albeit I have heard that story too.'

'So, I am being tested on my search for the Grail?' Hal tried to inject some humour into his own voice as he gestured to the chalice on the ledge. It was all a bit too much for him to take in right now and he truly feared for his sanity.

'Every man searches for the grail. It is the truth at the heart of every life. All set out on the journey but not many have the courage to continue looking, when they find themselves lost in the dark realms of their own souls.'

Hal shuddered. The cold was seeping through the wall and into his bones, and he had a sudden fear of remaining there until his own bones would have melded with the cave. As if reading his mind, the ghost spoke again, sounding unnervingly close this time.

'This was *my* destiny, not thine. Find the food thou hast in thy sack, and once thou hast taken some sustenance and rested, I will show thee where the cave meets the outer world, and if the Lord wills it so, there thou mayst climb to safety.'

'Maybe I'll just try to find that spot now ... sir,' Hal declared, pushing himself back onto his feet.

'Thou hast need of strength, Halliwell. Dost not heed the injury to my leg where I failed in mine own escape?' Gingerly moving closer, Hal examined the skeleton, and this time noticed that the right fibula was indeed badly broken. With an injury like that the old man would not have been able to walk more than a short distance, let alone scramble along whatever escape route he had found.

By now Hal was so exhausted that he doubted he would have been able to stagger any further if Hades himself had indeed been the occupier of the cave. With a shrug of resignation he filled his water bottle from the spring, moved a fair distance from the skeleton and searched for the chocolate in his rucksack. He forced himself to eat, leaving the energy bar for when he woke. He knew he must sleep now, however gruesome the idea of closing his eyes in the presence of the skeleton was. He would let the torch burn for as long as possible and then, once he woke, would have to hope his flashlight would last until he found the place where he could escape.

He laid his head on his bag. The thought of resting it on the rock, which would have a similar feel to the cold surface of the ancient bones, was impossible. He was unsure whether to lie facing the dead man, or with his back to him, but in the end settled for being able to keep his eye on the skeleton — what he could see being less frightening than what his imagination could supply. He felt almost drunk, struggling to hold on to his senses as they, inexorably, faded away. His last thought, before sleep claimed him, was how repellent he found the deformed skull.

'Rest well. I will keep watch over thee,' the sibilant voice reassured him.

'I am not at all sure that I find that comforting,' Hal muttered — then curled up on his side and slept.

17

Roseberry Topping

Leo woke feeling wonderfully refreshed, having slept better than he had for months, rocked by the subtle movements of the tide. Before he opened his eyes he was aware of a delicious combination of scents. Strongest was the aroma of coffee and toast emanating from the galley. How disappointing, he mused, that he had missed watching Angelina wake and slide those long legs out of bed. However, there was an underlying scent of her in the cabin, a light, heady mixture of perfume and warm skin, which made him smile as he inhaled deeply. Before leaving the cabin he ran a hand over her neatly folded pyjamas and then, feeling slightly guilty at the turn his thoughts were taking, went to splash cold water on his face and make himself presentable.

When he had dressed and joined her in the galley, Leo was pleased to see that Angelina had got her sea-legs at last. Her skin no longer had a green hue to it; in fact she was slightly flushed with the effort of trying to boil water for the coffee. She was muttering to herself, exasperated at having to go on deck, locate the rear locker that housed the gas and open the taps there, before being able to use the hob. She was wearing a loose grey cardigan over a toning T-shirt and jeans which were enchantingly tight in all the right places. Leo sat at the table so that he was at the perfect level for admiring the stitching across her back pockets. What a wonderful way to start a day!

'I was thinking about where to go today,' Angelina said, handing him a cup of instant coffee and turning back to the toast. Leo got up to fetch some sugar. The cardigan was soft and warm as he brushed past her. He usually took his coffee black, but this morning decided that milk was needed, since that allowed him to repeat the manoeuvre. Angelina was concentrating on the bread she was trying to toast in a frying pan. As she pushed her hair behind her ears, Leo saw that the tips of her ears were slightly pink — with exertion or embarrassment he was not sure — but he did not think she had objected to their brief contact. He reached around her, took down two plates from a cupboard over the sink and held them out for her to slide the toast onto. He, at least, appreciated the lesser-known advantages brought by the cramped confines of a small boat!

Taking a seat next to him, Angelina sipped her coffee and pulled a face.

'How can anyone enjoy living like this? I am covered in bruises, you snored all night—' (Leo looked abashed at this) '—and Hal doesn't have a coffee machine or even a toaster!' she exclaimed.

'This bread is toasted to perfection, in any case,' Leo reassured her. 'However, I agree about the coffee. On *Elisir* I would have made it for you in my little mokka machine, using the best Italian coffee. Or I could have taken you to the bar and ordered a frothy cappuccino and a warm croissant.'

Angelina smiled at him, obviously not averse to the idea of breakfasting with him another time, and Leo felt his heart jerk unexpectedly, lowering his eyes quickly to mask his emotions as he industriously spread strawberry jam.

'Grace is going to keep looking for Hal near Thirsk, so I thought we could drive to a place where he took me once to walk. I can't think of anything else to do. I keep hoping that Hal will phone and all this worry will have been for nothing. There is a nice pub in Great Ayton village where we may as well have lunch afterwards, if we have not found him by then. He just might be there — maybe he sprained an ankle and there is no phone reception or something. Anyway, it's Hal's kind of place because it is high and involves a climb, albeit a relatively gentle one and .... I need to be doing *something,* even if it turns out to be useless.'

'I especially like the idea of a pub lunch,' Leo reassured her with a serene smile, then covered her hand with his, thinking how fragile the bones in those long slim fingers felt.

'We will find Hal, or Grace will, and he will be OK,' he assured her. Angelina turned her hand in his and gave it a slight squeeze before letting go and picking up her coffee again.

'It is an odd shaped hill. You can see it standing up like a volcanic cone for miles as you drive over the moorland. I can't remember the route exactly, so I am glad I have my sat nav,' She got up to fetch her handbag from the cabin and rummaged around in it until she found the device, then handed it to Leo, who in the meantime had finished his toast, saying, 'Can you set the destination as Roseberry Topping, please?'

Leo snorted and almost choked on his coffee. Looking up through watering eyes he saw that Angelina was laughing too.

'Oh, how I love these English names,' he said, imagining a cake-shaped hill topped with whipped cream and a jaunty cherry on top.

The reality was very different. As they drove through the country lanes, hemmed in alternately with hedges and wild moor, Leo thought how dissimilar this land was to the Italian countryside, with its fertile fields of sweetcorn and sunflowers, and hills covered in vineyards and olive groves. This morning a weak sun was peeking timidly around ominous black clouds that hunkered down over the landscape. Leo was glad he had his rain jacket as well as his yellow jumper, because the summer morning that had greeted them when they left the boat had felt like mid-winter to him. Angelina had scoffed, but he noticed that she had pulled the collar of her own jacket close at the neck as she strode towards the harbour car park.

Angelina was making an effort to drive slowly today, and given the number of sharp, blind bends, Leo was very grateful. She had turned on the radio; Leo suspected that she now regretted talking so much about herself the previous day and was taking no chances of that today. He smiled to himself, empathising with the contradictory sentiments of the love song that was playing. '*I'm not in love, so don't forget it ... It's just a silly phase, I'm going through ...*'

'I have no idea why I talked so much to you yesterday, about Hal and our past,' Angelina said pensively, changing gears as she headed into yet another corner.

'I think we are similar in some ways, my dear,' Leo replied, wondering if she had read his mind. He turned to admire her sharp profile. 'We've spent a lifetime building barriers around ourselves, as if we could protect our hearts in that way.'

'True.' Angelina nodded. 'But that still doesn't explain why I opened up to *you*.'

'Perhaps,' Leo suggested quietly, 'because we are becoming friends?'

She flashed him a sardonic smile but did not deny his words.

'There it is!' she said, indicating ahead, and Leo turned to see a most extraordinary hill. It was probably not very high, certainly not a mountain and yet, standing out so drastically from the flat moorland surrounding it, its half-cone shape and craggy cliff top was impressive.

'That jagged bit at the top was caused by a geological fault or maybe a mining collapse in the early 1900s. They used to mine for ironstone and jet round here,' Angelina informed him. 'And I have even heard people comparing it to the Matterhorn,' she continued, flicking glances at him to enjoy his reaction to this outrageous exaggeration.

Leo raised an eyebrow at her. 'Indeed, it's very like the Mattrehorn, just as it is a long distance to drive from London to Liverpool, British plumbing makes sense and the food is the best in the world,' he assured her, absurdly happy to have been responsible for making her chuckle.

Some time later, when they were still walking through a pretty wood on the path that led from the car park to the summit, Leo was a little less sure about the hill's dimensions. It looked much bigger and never seemed to get any closer. However, the walking was easy — if a little muddy in places — and the air smelt wonderful, of damp earth and fresh leaves. Great clumps of bluebells covered the ground between the oaks; the flowers were finished at this time of year but must have formed a spectacular blue carpet in the spring. A woodpecker worked diligently somewhere hidden in the leafy canopy, and Angelina told him that she and Hal had seen a small group of roe deer on their walk. All in all, Leo was thoroughly enjoying himself. The path was narrow enough in places that Angelina's arm brushed his, and he had been able to offer his hand around a few of those well-placed muddy spots. There had been little need to help her, since her legs could take her across more easily than his, but she had raised no objections. Then again, maybe she thought *she* had been helping *him*, Leo mused.

Hal's car had not been in the car park, but Angelina had said he often parked in the village near the pub or in some other remote space, so that he could walk further and avoid the tourists who flocked here on sunny days. Leo was aware that Angelina also believed this walk to be a waste of time, but understood that she needed to keep busy, and he had no objections. The weather was quite pleasant now, away from the strong coastal wind. He had even undone his jacket to let the breeze cool him once they left the trees, turning onto a stone path that skirted the wood and then through a small gate and onto Roseberry Common.

Angelina had avoided the steeper route that would have taken them to the top a bit more quickly, because she remembered it had played havoc with her thigh muscles when Hal had taken her up there before. Instead, they were meandering gently uphill along a well-worn path through grassland. There was no heather growing here, but further below, the moorland was purpled with great expanses of it. The views were already spectacular: a tapestry of green fields dotted with villages, and far off a larger city, which Angelina thought was Middlesbrough. In the distance, when the heavy clouds shifted enough, they caught glimpses of the coastline and dull pewter sea.

As they walked, Angelina told him snippets of local history. She started each of these bits of folklore with the words 'Hal told me ...' and Leo realised that it was her way of feeling connected to him. He nodded and made encouraging noises while keeping his breath for the steeper climb ahead, but was genuinely interested to hear that the area had been inhabited since the Bronze Age — the odd name of the hill came from the Viking expression for Odin's Rock — and that James Cook had liked to climb up here as a young lad.

Interested though he was, Leo's attention wandered somewhat when two pretty girls came into sight, approaching downhill at a brisk rate which made their ponytails, and other parts of their anatomy, bounce in a very attractive way. They were dressed in walking shorts — which Leo thought highly inappropriate, considering the weather — but very enjoyable nevertheless.

'Morning,' the blonde one in the lead called cheerfully, stopping for her friend to catch up. Leo wished them a very good morning too, then glanced at Angelina's face and decided not to engage in a lengthy conversation in case he risked ruining the friendly atmosphere that had blossomed between them.

'Better keep an eye on the weather,' said the girl in a slightly breathless voice. 'Looks like it might take a turn for the worse soon, so if you want to reach the top you'd better hurry.'

Leo glanced at the sky. There was a good bit of sunshine showing between the clouds, so he was surprised by the girl's pessimistic forecast. Usually he found the English altogether too cheerful about the weather. They would say things like 'should clear up in a bit' when there was nothing but glowering, rain-laden cloud to be seen, and would greet each other with a friendly 'bit fresh today' when it was cold enough to freeze a man before he had time to pull his gloves on.

With another flash of healthy teeth, the girls set off again. Enjoying the pause from the climb and the splendid view of pert, retreating buttocks, Leo politely watched to make sure they were coping well with the descent. They were. Pale legs gleamed between sturdy boots and shorts which fitted their curves tidily. Angelina cleared her throat. She gave him a look that would have shrivelled the necessary attributes of many a strong man, muttered something and stomped off.

Leo, then bravely carried on. Since he was already in the doghouse, he let Angelina put a bit of distance between them before following. He found this view even more pleasant than the last, but refrained from telling her.

Trudging behind Angelina, who seemed tireless, Leo thought that it was a good job this was an easy climb, as their footwear was not suitable at all. He was wearing his boat shoes, and he had seen Angelina hesitate over an expensive-looking pair of brown court shoes with good sized heels, although in the end she had plumped for suede loafers, for which he was quite glad as that brought her slightly closer to his own height.

Leo turned his attention to the landscape. There was nothing soft about it, just grass, rock and sky. The surrounding moors were dotted with sheep, and the path they followed was strewn with currant-like rabbit droppings. He felt very alien and far away from his homeland, and amused himself by imagining showing Angelina the places he loved, taking her walking along sandy beaches or driving with her into the hills around Rome with their castles and fortified towns, where they would eat delicious local dishes and drink the fine white wines of the area.

His stomach gave a loud grumble of reproach at the thought of food and he hurried to catch up. The sooner they reached the summit, the sooner they would be able to call it a day and head off to the pub. The last bit of the climb left them both breathless. The rock underfoot was uneven and the sheer drop of cliff, formed by the large rock fall Angelina had mentioned, was somewhat daunting when Leo considered that it had been caused by a geological fault as much as by the mining. Still, everything felt very steady right then, apart from his ragged breathing.

He really must stop smoking, he thought, sitting thankfully on a cold slab and shaking out a cigarette. He was dragging on it therapeutically when a small shaggy mongrel ran up to him. Its owner was nowhere in sight and it obviously wanted company.

***

Angelina stood some distance away, getting her breath back and struggling to rid herself of the jealousy that had bothered her ever since she had noticed Leo being so obviously charmed by the two young walkers. She had always known that she was not pretty, and had hardened herself to the fact over the years, making the most of the good points that she did possess, in order to become polished and stylish instead. However, there were moments when she wished for the softness and curves that men enjoyed. She was irritated with *herself*, not him. For some reason, she had begun to think that Leo was attracted to her, and her intrinsic honesty forced her to acknowledge that she was not at all impervious to him either. Why that should be was a mystery to her. He was certainly not what one could call a good-looking man, and yet … there was something very attractive in his rich, well-modulated voice and the way his face crinkled when he smiled, which he had been doing surprisingly often in the last two days. Also, he made her laugh. Most importantly, he made her remember that she was a woman.

As they had walked through the oak wood earlier she had been astonished at how young and light-hearted she had felt, enjoying the touch of Leo's hand on hers as he helped her around muddy puddles, holding on a little longer than he needed to once they were past the obstacles. Then those girls had brought her back to reality sharply. She felt foolish and consequently was covering it up with her usual haughty manner. She was *fifty-two*, for heaven's sake! She was lucky to have the kind of metabolism that did not encourage fat to stick around, but knew that men were not at all averse to a bit of padding in the right places. Her sallow skin was coarsening and her hair was quite grey. She could not imagine that there was much about her that would attract a man these days.

Swallowing down her hurt, she watched in growing fascination as Leo underwent an unexpected transformation. The somewhat morose figure, hunched inside his jacket as he smoked, face crumpled in weary resignation, had disappeared and he was laughing enthusiastically. He had stubbed the cigarette out and was down on his knees with the dog, which was squirming on its back, legs paddling ecstatically in the air as Leo tickled its tummy. After a few minutes of this close bonding, Leo began to sneeze violently and sat back on the rock.

'Are you all right, Mr Marconi?' Angelina asked, taking refuge behind their earlier formality to cover up her conflicting emotions of irritation and mirth. Leo blew his nose loudly on a pristine handkerchief he had found in his pocket, and said something incomprehensible. The dog put a paw onto his new friend's knee and was rewarded by an affectionate pat. Looking up, Leo repeated his last remark.

'I said, I am allergic to dogs,' he said, and grinned rather sheepishly.

'What on earth are you doing rolling around like a schoolboy with one then?'

'Because I love them. They are much nicer than human beings, in general.' Leo shook his head regretfully, adding, 'It seems that I have a tendency to like all the things that are not good for me: wine, cigarettes, dogs…!'

A shrill whistle from the other side of the summit sent the dog off, little legs bounding through the bracken and its plume of a tail spiralling madly. Angelina tended to agree with Leo. On the whole, she too found dogs to be better companions than humans, and would have loved one if only she did not have to be out of the house all day.

They wandered over to peer down at the rock fall. The view from the top was well worth the effort of the climb, although the wind was much sharper here, exposed as they were, and Angelina wished she had worn another layer of clothing. It was obvious that Hal was not up here, though neither of them mentioned it. Leo was still sneezing sporadically, although he assured her that he would be fine once he had washed his hands.

'I remember that Hal told me about a well up here, somewhere close. Let's see if we can find it, for heaven's sake,' she said, moving away to hide her amusement – she was still cross with him and not prepared to let go of that yet. She clambered down the rocks and along a path to the north. She could see three dots in the distance, the dog and his owners heading for the village. A faint rumble from her stomach reminded her that it was almost lunchtime. Looking up, she saw with some surprise that the girls had been right — the weather was changing fast, with dark clouds brooding menacingly above.

She found the well she had been looking for only because the vegetation around it was greener than its surroundings. The well was dry, just a slab of rock surrounded by moss and small plants. She remembered a legend that said some young prince had once drowned here, but there was no sense of melancholy now and it seemed impossible that there had ever been enough water to cause such a death. She doubted that Leo would even find enough to wash his hands, although maybe wiping them in the damp moss would do.

Where was he? she wondered — and turned just in time to see him careening down the hillside toward her. He looked strangely joyous, arms outstretched as he let gravity pull him onwards. Then he saw her and tried to change his trajectory. He was going too fast, though, and barrelled into her, grabbing her around the waist and spinning her with him. His head was pressed to her breast as they staggered around as if dancing. She held on to him as they circled, and he looked up at her, eyes creased in a blissful smile. The twinkle in them made her think that maybe he did not find her bosom such an unsubstantial pillow as it undoubtedly was. Tripping over a boulder, they collapsed in a tangle of limbs, his apologies lost amid their laughter.

'Mr Marconi, what *were* you doing?' she managed to say at last, pulling away and trying to straighten her clothes.

'Running, my dear. I felt a remarkable urge to run downhill like a boy, and by the time I realised you were in my way I was going too fast to avoid our ... delightful collision.'

Angelina was feeling breathless again, and it had nothing to do with the physical exertion. She indicated the spring and suggested, rather more sharply than she had intended, that he try to clean his hands. He did not look in the least rebuked as he went over to investigate. In fact, he could almost be described as chirpy, which was such a drastic alteration from his usual lugubrious demeanour that she was disconcerted.

'Aah, maybe I will not need to worry about the lack of water here, after all,' Leo commented, as rain began to speckle the rocks. They looked up. There was no trace of sun now and the rain was falling faster. Leo raised a brow inquiringly.

'Might this be a good time to retire to that pub you spoke of for some lunch, do you think?'

18

A Prickly Escape

Hal pulled Grace toward him, his fingers deep in the springy coils of her close-cropped hair. Her skin radiated heat. The elegant bones of her skull were hard beneath firm flesh. He opened his mouth to kiss her — then jerked away as the bones turned cold and the flesh dissolved into milky, misshapen growths, her beautiful dark eyes replaced by the gaping hollows in the old man's skull.

Shivering uncontrollably, Hal found himself awake – again. This was definitely the most horrible night he had ever spent. He had fallen asleep in exhaustion, only to find himself inside nightmares that sent him shuddering awake numerous times. His torch had burnt out hours ago and the darkness was complete. He knew that the ghost's skeleton lay a few feet away from him, but could see nothing at all. Once or twice he had flicked on his flashlight for a moment of comfort, and each time he did so, the view of ancient bones dismayed him anew.

During the lucid moments of sleeplessness throughout this tormented night, Hal had found himself facing a few unwelcome facts about himself. The ghost's words, about every man being on a journey to find his true nature, had had a strong impact on him. He realised that, for most of his life, instead of searching for inner truth, he had been running from it. Once convinced that he had given himself completely to Grace, he now saw the falseness of that belief. Certain as he was of his love for her, nevertheless he had been holding a part of himself back, stopping short of real commitment.

He had always made his way through life with a light tread, finding the humour in things and seeking only that which that gave him pleasure, following the philosophy which said 'if it feels good — do it!' This way of life, of turning his back on a so-called 'normal' existence, was yet another way of running from responsibility.

It took courage to look at himself and face his own shadows, as the ghost had done. Now, Hal realised that he had always had a deep fear of abandonment. He had felt death treading at his heels from childhood onwards. Losing his parents together like that had been traumatic, but he had refused to acknowledge it as a boy, and as he grew older he had set out to challenge life, almost daring death to take him too.

Grace had overwhelmed him with her beauty, which ran far deeper than the physical. She had tried to show him the way that she saw life; that the best moment one could ever have was the precise instant that one was living through, and to give oneself to it joyfully. She had shown him that one could take those moments, enrich them with happy memories and enhance them with joyful hope. Above all, she was at peace with herself — and maybe it was that which drew Hal to her, because it was a quality he had never experienced in himself.

What Hal had come to realise, in this vast, overwhelming darkness, was that he had been fighting himself forever. Well then, he decided, maybe this was the moment to really change. Could he continue his journey without shrinking from the shadows as they came, but instead face up to them, learn from them and let peace find him?

Hal slowly became aware that there was a difference in the cavern. It was no longer pitch black. A soft burgeoning light was inching across the cave floor from a fissure in the wall just beyond the skeleton. It was morning now, and that must be the way out that the ghost had mentioned. Hal did not think he had ever been so relieved to see the dawn.

Standing up, stiff from his night on the cold floor and aching from his injuries, Hal made his way toward the light. There was a crack in the cave wall above shoulder height that led to a slim ledge. Above the ledge was a passage, so steep as to be almost sheer. It was narrow and lined with jagged spurs of rock which he doubted he would be able to squeeze past easily. At the very top, some thirty or so feet above, light filtered through thick undergrowth of some kind. It would not be an easy climb.

Grateful that he had some food left, because he had got his appetite back with a vengeance, Hal fetched the energy bar and his water bottle, breakfasting on them as he studied the passage. The longer he looked, the more daunting it seemed. At least he felt a bit better this morning, in spite of his restless night. The light-headed sensation had gone. He had not heard the ghostly voice yet this morning either, he thought, glancing over at the skeleton, its jaw open in a grotesque parody of a grin. For the first time, he noticed a small chest next to the body. Closer examination showed that its wood was quite rotten and the metal clasp rusted half away.

'Hope you don't mind, my friend,' Hal said to the skeleton as he sprang the lock. The lid opened with a groan and splintering of wood, revealing its disintegrating contents. Inside, there were several crude glass bottles. Hal wondered what they had contained. Herbs perhaps, or poison? There was a slight rustle behind him and the dust in the chest stirred as if disturbed by a breeze. Hairs rose all over Hal's body, with the uncanny certainty that his invisible companion was breathing down his neck. Sure enough, the voice was back.

'Poison, aye. It was easier than the other option that faced me once I broke my leg trying to climb up yonder. There was water a-plenty but very little food. No ... I did not much like the idea of a long drawn-out death by starvation, although ... some say tis a sin to take one's own life ...'

The voice faded, as if the unseen soul was still pondering his sins. Hal's skin crawled at the thought of having to make such a decision, to choose one's own manner of death. Ignoring the potentially lethal bottles, Hal carefully lifted up a small piece of what appeared to be the moon-milk that formed the macabre decoration around the cave and rolled it around in his hand.

''Twas for yon crystal that I found myself buried here, young Halliwell. I used it as a cure for acid of the stomach and as a tonic for the heart. I was known in the area as a healer. Tis a profession with little comfort — if all goes well thou art lauded but if aught goes wrong, well ... thou art to blame.'

The voice had moved from behind him and now seemed to emanate from the very spot where the old bones lay. Hal gazed at the dark depressions where the old man's eyes once would have been. It seemed important that he look at them respectfully as he listened to the fate of the long-forgotten healer.

'There was a sickness in the village where I lived. Many died. I did what I could but 'twas not enough. My fault was in mine own survival ... so I decided to leave for a while, until the anger that sprang from desperate grief had lessened. I knew these tunnels well because I came here often to gather the rock. I had a sturdy ladder in the outer cave, the spot where thee flew down to join me.'

The ghost stopped to wheeze with laughter. Hal shook his head. His spectre seemed to have a rather warped sense of humour. When it carried on, the voice seemed almost gleefully restored by the image of Hal's body plummeting down, to destroy centuries of solitude.

'Over the years I had established a pathway of torches, in sconces I had carved, to light me to this, the most holy of places. Little did I suspect it would become my grave. The headman lost a son to the sickness. He thought I was to blame and had me closed within this place. How could I reproach him?

'So many times have I pondered on this - why could I not find a cure? Why must I, old and stooped with age, not be claimed when that rosy-cheeked child was, along with his mother and half the village? These are questions that I must ask myself time and again ... Centuries of asking and no answers.'

The voice died away to a whisper. Hal was surprised to find that his cheeks were damp, and brushed the tears away with a sleeve. His sadness crushed the breath in his lungs and he longed to offer some words of comfort, but could think of none. He reached out and gently touched the cold scapula as he would have patted the shoulder if the old man had been alive and standing before him.

'Heed well my words: learn to love thyself, lad, just as thou art. Is it not written in the Good Book that we are to love others as ourselves, and so does it not follow that we must first love ourselves? And if we forgive the trespasses of others, must we not also forgive ourselves our own trespasses? Judge not, that ye be not judged, saith the Lord. All this I struggled mightily to learn during my life, but since then I have had ample time to absorb the lesson well.' Hal thought he heard a smile in the whisper. The words sounded vaguely familiar, but Hal had last looked in a Bible at school and he could not exactly place them.

'Unconditional love, I think that's called,' he muttered under his breath.

The old man chuckled breathily again, and said, 'Thou hast it right, young Halliwell, though thy fashion of putting it is barbaric to my ear.'

Then, restraining the involuntary shudder that touching the body had triggered, Hal turned his attention back to his escape route. He stared up the passage again, noting that the light was brighter than before. It illuminated the difficulties all too clearly; sheer rock alternating with outcrops that narrowed the passage so that it would be hard to get past. Still, looking at it was not going to get him out. He would leave his rucksack behind, as it would only hinder him if it snagged on the rocks. The same went for his water bottle, so he had better drink his fill before starting the climb.

Taking up the little metal chalice, Hal dipped it into the holy well. He raised it in an odd toast to the skeleton before drinking deeply, then replaced it on its ledge.

'Thank you,' he said with heartfelt gratitude — and felt a brief cold grip on his own shoulder, as if in farewell.

The wall below the ledge was regrettably smooth. Hal reached up and took hold of the edge and then, every muscle in his aching body shrieking in protest, hauled himself upwards. His legs scrabbled helplessly, trying to find some purchase, to no avail. He collapsed back onto the cavern floor, frustrated at being thwarted so quickly. He was still weaker than he had thought, his muscles stiff and his bruised ribs painful. However, if he did not get out of here his fate was all too obvious, the grisly reminder stretched out by the cave wall nearby. Hal resolved to do it next time. All he had to do was focus his strength. Once he had regained his breath he took a few steps back, then made a running start that allowed him to jump a little higher. This time he almost got onto the ledge. He managed to get one elbow up, but the ledge was too narrow and he was too big to be able to manoeuvre properly.

Suddenly his foot found a firm grip and he was able to push the rest of his body up. Taking a shaky breath, he looked over the edge to confirm what he had seen before. There *was* no foothold on that stretch of wall, none at all. So that meant .... ? It made Hal's head spin to think about it, so he simply didn't.

'If I may save one soul ... *thy* soul, Halliwell, perchance I will find peace.'

Those words echoed in Hal's mind as he climbed, feet and hands slipping on sharp rock and scrabbling in the thin layer of dirt that had fallen into the passage over the years. Buoyed up by the words, he somehow squeezed his way past each overhang, oblivious to the rips in his clothes and the pain in his fingers as he fought for a grip.

Finally he was there, inches from safety. All that remained was the great bush that grew across the entrance, its thick roots an easy handhold to haul him up the last stretch. He breathed in deeply, feeling inebriated by the clean, fresh air. A gentle rain wet his upturned face. Safety at last!

Then he faltered. A closer look confirmed his suspicion — he was underneath a gorse bush. The sweet-scented yellow flowers glittered in the rain surrounded by countless savage little thorns.

As Hal braced himself for a prickly rebirth into the world, he could have sworn he heard soft laughter wheezing from the cavern below.

19

The Summer House

The rain pelted down in huge droplets that soaked through their trousers before they had covered more than a hundred yards. Angelina pulled her hood up, but the wind kept blowing it off again. There was no shelter up on the summit, and the rain-slicked rocks were already treacherously slippery as they made their way cautiously across them. It seemed quite dark in spite of being just past mid-day, the clouds a solid dark blanket overhead.

'Summer in England!' Leo remarked caustically. His curls were slicked wetly across his head and he looked quite miserable. Remembering his reluctance to go out in the rain when she had shown him the last house he had found fault with, Angelina imagined that if she kept taking him out in such inclement weather he would decide to find another estate agent. That thought made her realise just how much she would miss him if she never saw him again, and her spirits sank even lower. As if to confirm her sensation of impending doom, lightning slashed over the moors and a deep growl of thunder reverberated through them.

'Thor, I suppose, come to visit his father's sacred hill,' Angelina quipped, giving up the fight with her hood as its toggles lashed her in the eye again. She pushed them down the front of her jacket, cursing the rain that slithered in with them, and let the hood flap wildly against her shoulders.

'*Per dio, chi me l'ha fatto fare? Avrei potuto essere in una bella spiaggia, con un sole caldo, e invece sono qui, in questo posto dimenticato da dio…*'

Pushing into the wind as they staggered along side by side, Angelina had no idea what the torrent of Italian meant, but thought she could probably imagine. What a very beautiful language it was, though, even when muttered angrily under the breath. She searched for a sign of the storm lessening, but found only that the horizon was alarmingly close, visibility cut back drastically by the driving rain. Leo grabbed her arm and shouted something, pointing downhill. She screwed up her eyes, trying to make out what it was he was pointing at, and eventually saw the shape of what appeared to be a small building.

They left the path and scrambled down the hill, feet slipping and twisting over mounds of grass and unexpected dips. All she needed now, Angelina thought, was to put her foot in a rabbit hole and sprain an ankle. Her jeans were so waterlogged that they were sliding down around her hips and made a nasty squelching noise each time she hauled them up again. Her jacket was not up to this kind of treatment and had sprung leaks, especially around the neck and shoulders. She kept her head down so that her hair formed some kind of barrier between the rain and her nose, but then had to flip it back and raise her head every few steps to make sure they were heading in the right direction.

Another crash of thunder was shockingly loud and she gasped. Leo, a bit further ahead, heard her and stopped. He held out his hand and she grasped it thankfully as they began to run. Never mind the rabbit holes, being fried by lightening seemed a much worse threat.

They were almost at the building before she realised what it was. She had seen photos of the pale-stone building with its domed roof, some kind of summer house or shooting-lodge. Whatever it had been built for, she was glad to see that it was decorated by a sturdy metal weather-vane on top. She wondered if that would work as a lightening conductor, but realised that her knowledge was hazy on this point. Feeling slightly reassured by that thought she followed Leo through the open doorway just as another flash brightened the gloom, thunder booming out seconds later.

Inside the summer-house it was still chilly as the wind drove the rain through the empty window spaces, but there was a patch by the old chimney that was a little drier, so they huddled there, shivering. Eventually Leo moved away, shook his head violently until his curls began to unfurl again, and then unzipped his jacket and shrugged it off.

'Take yours off too, Angelina,' he ordered, and when she had struggled out of it, wrapped his around her. She had known immediately that it was an item of quality. It was properly waterproofed, and inside was only a little damp and wonderfully warm from his body. She closed her eyes for a second, enjoying the very masculine scent of smoke and aftershave that clung to the jacket, and murmured her thanks. Laying her own flimsy jacket over the hearth, Leo sat down by the fireplace and leant back. The yellow jumper looked very bright and comforting in the shadowy light as she sat next to him.

'I knew I shouldn't have left my bag in the car,' Leo said despondently.

'Why, don't tell me you had some food hidden away in it,' Angelina said, her stomach rumbling loudly at the thought.

Leo shook his head regretfully.

'No food — but I did have some very good bottles of Montalcino wine, which would have alleviated the discomfort somewhat, don't you think?'

Angelina smiled and wriggled a little closer, wrapping Leo's jacket partially over him too. That seemed to remind him of something, for he turned and began to delve into the damp pockets. She had no idea what he was looking for, but it was nicely warming being so close to the yellow jumper and she fought back an urge to bury her cold nose in it.

'There, I knew I had put them here!' He offered her one of the foil-covered chocolate mints that they had been given with coffee in the restaurant the previous evening. While they munched in companionable silence, Angelina reached over and felt through her own pockets. All she came up with was a lint covered Polo mint, which Leo nobly allowed her to eat all by herself.

'It's ironic, really. We set out to look for Hal, and even though I knew he would not be up here, I dragged you along anyway. Now it looks like we are stuck here ourselves. Who knows how long this storm will last.'

The mention of Hal started Angelina worrying again. As the thunder rolled and grumbled slightly further away, she had a sudden image of it moving on, lightning slashing the moors and crags, seeking out her brother — wherever he was. What if he really *was* hurt somewhere? If he had fallen, as Grace had thought, and was lying out in this storm where no one could find him? What if this time he was *really* in trouble?

She was jolted out of her unpleasant thoughts as Leo moved unexpectedly nearer, whispered a phrase in Italian that sounded lovely, and slid his arm around her.

'*L'amor che move il sole e l'altre stelle.*'

'What?' Angelina squeaked, as Leo pulled her head toward his pullover and blithely translated for her. As if he did not know what she meant, she fumed angrily, torn between the need to shove him away and the desire to let her head rest exactly where it was, because it felt incredibly right in the warm curve of his shoulder.

'It's Dante. It means, the love that moves the sun and the other stars.'

'Not what does it mean! What are you doing?' she demanded, jerking upright.

'Sharing my body warmth with you. My survival manual said that was what one should do in circumstances like this.' Angelina could hear the smile in his voice and felt her own lips twitch too. He snuggled her closer and murmured into her wet hair, 'Of course, it is always better if the body to share with is that of a lovely lady.'

Angelina pushed him away, saying sharply, 'Pity those hikers aren't here then!'

Leo studied her bedraggled face for a moment and smiled gently, smoothing her cheek with his thumb.

'My dear, how you underestimate yourself.' His voice was seductively mellow and it really was deliciously warming so close to him. Angelina ran her hand through her hair, sending a small shower of drips over them both, and tried to be angry. It was her last defence, and she needed one. Almost shouting, she began to list her faults. 'Maybe you could tell me exactly what it is you find lovely? I am tall, and skinny —

Leo interrupted her, stroking her wet knee. 'Yes,' he agreed, 'you are too tall for a woman and have far too many sharp corners to be cuddly.'

'I know, I have no curves at all.' To her surprise Leo, instead of being put off by this, moved his hand up to her breast and curved his fingers around it, nodding.

'Very small breasts, I agree.' Both his hands began to move now, moulding themselves to her contours as he continued his examination.

'Slender waist.' He slid his fingers under her T-shirt and ran them up the long curve of her spine and then down again, leaving her quite breathless. So, she had not been imagining the attraction between them after all. He really did find her desirable, she realised, and felt the ice she had nurtured deep within her for so long begin to melt.

'Scrawny bottom,' His next comment was outrageous. There was nothing wrong at all with her bottom and Angelina told him so, shifting until her weight pressed him down, and they slid along the wall to lie next to each other on the dusty floor. He moved his hands down again, curving his fingers around her buttocks.

'Indeed, there is nothing wrong here at all,' Leo admitted, his breath catching slightly and his voice hoarse. He raised himself on his side so that he could look down at her with smouldering dark eyes, then he slowly glided his hands back up across her firm stomach. Angelina thought that the heat building between them would have their clothes dry in no time at this rate. Warm fingers smoothing the silk and lace at her breast turned her liquid inside.

'Small they might be but extremely pleasant to hold,' he declared, and lowered his head to kiss her. She kissed him right back and went on kissing him as her fingers began their own search.

At the touch of her lips Leo felt an overwhelming hunger consume him. Angelina! The only hunger he could remember in the last few years had been that for his next glass of wine, which he had used to numb his emotions instead of setting them on fire. He had been so reliant on the props of alcohol and cigarettes that he had forgotten to live. Now, with this marvellous woman moulding herself to him, his past seemed stale and uninteresting. In his arms Angelina was surprisingly and pleasantly softer than Leo had imagined. True, he winced when her knee met his thigh, but her angularity seemed to have melted into delightful femininity. He almost wondered if it was truly her and pulled away, peering into the shadows to make sure. Lightning helpfully lit up the room but it was her words that reassured him most,

'This is absolutely *not* the time to demonstrate that you are a gentleman, Leonardo.'

'Quite right,' he agreed, and gathered her back into his arms with a smile.

20

The Sense of Grace

Grace slipped out of the guest house, hoping that she would not have disturbed her kind landlady too much with her early departure. There had been a chorus of multi-toned woofs from the back of the house though, that she rather doubted Mrs Wuz would have slept through. She was glad that she had thought to pay her bill the previous night so that she did not have to hang around now. She couldn't have stayed in bed any longer. She had woken in the half-light before dawn, from a dream where she had felt as if she was in Hal's body, breathing with him, and had known that he was thinking of her. Then the pleasant connection had been cut abruptly and she had jerked awake, her last grisly image that of a skull with sparse teeth jutting up from the gaping mandible. In spite of the gruesome picture it had made, she had been more puzzled than scared by the sight. Where on earth could Hal be?

Climbing into the Land Rover, she sent a brief text to Angelina, letting her know that she was going to start searching for Hal nearby. It was too early to ring and disturb her and Leonardo. It was never too early for her grandma though. The old lady was a light sleeper, but more than that, there had never been a moment when she had not seemed to know that Grace needed her, sometimes even before Grace herself knew it. Fondling the cross at her neck in a habitual gesture, Grace dialled the number.

'*There* you are, child,' Grandma Clair answered immediately. 'I suppose you didn't sleep much, did you? Have you had breakfast?' Thatcher screeched something and laughed raucously in the background. Grace could picture the two of them, Grandma Clair sitting in bed, with her purple shawl across her shoulders, and Thatcher perched above her on the brass bedstead. The bird had his own cage where he slept, but the door was usually left open for him to come and go as he pleased. Grace smiled, instantly restored by the warmth in her Grandma's voice as she scolded her for leaving without eating anything. Then, with one of her sudden changes of direction, the old lady's tone changed.

'I saw Hal, briefly, last night.' Grandma Clair hesitated and then asked, 'Did you know that he is not alone, Gracie?' Without waiting for a reply, she continued as if she had seen Grace's nod, 'Yes I thought so .... I'm glad I am not there, child. That is one cold and dark place.'

Thinking of her own sensations, Grace was not surprised by the words. Finishing up the conversation with promises to ring as soon as she had any news, Grace placed her hands on the steering wheel and took several long, deep breaths as she concentrated on opening up to her inner instincts. While not religious in the conventional sense, she believed strongly in a universal connection which not everyone was aware of but which ran through all things. She sometimes wondered if this was what other people knew as God; some time she would look into that but for now, all she knew was that it was undoubtedly an underlying force of enormous power. She rarely went to church except to accompany Grandma Clair to the service on Christmas Eve, but Grace's faith in this force was strong.

Reaching out with her mind, she conjured an image of Hal and waited until she began to feel a vague tingling sensation, a sense of being pulled toward him. She did not judge her feelings or even try to understand them, because she had discovered long ago that this helped to dispel any pain or confusion that might surround them.

The light gradually brightened as she drove, slowly painting colour back into the dew-sparkled fields, and the russet bracken and yellow gorse that flamed in the hedges. It was overcast, and a closeness in the air made her think a storm was brewing. She drove through pretty Sutton-under-Whitestonecliffe and up the steep curves of Sutton Bank, and then, shortly after passing the visitor centre at the top, she turned left, no longer trying to think about where Hal might be with her rational mind but rather just holding on to the sense of him, and moving in that direction. It was far easier to do when sitting still and meditating than when trying to be aware of traffic at the same time. There were not many cars around this early on a Sunday, but nevertheless she needed to concentrate. Fortunately she had got used to the feel of Charlie's Land Rover by now, and found it easy to judge the width as she proceeded along the narrow country road she found herself on. About a quarter of an hour later she came to the spectacular ruins of Rievaulx Abbey. She had visited it some time ago with Hal on a sunny day in the spring, but they had approached it from the other direction so she had not recognised the road until now.

She pulled the Land Rover onto a grassy verge in front of the abbey and turned off the engine. It was such a beautiful place, nestled deep in the green valley. It seemed an incongruous location for what had obviously once been a splendid building, with its soaring stone walls and intricate arches, as if the Cistercian monks who had built it had wanted to keep its beauty hidden from the world, to be admired by themselves and God alone. Grace got out of the Land Rover and leant on its bonnet as she admired the abbey. She felt very different today. The fear that had been clogging her mind was less acute, and she was able to let her instinct guide her once more. This tranquil setting was exactly what she needed to help her energy and she closed her eyes, smiling as the fresh morning scents of damp grass and slowly warming earth surrounded her. It was not cold, and although the breeze that sent the clouds scampering across the sky was strong enough to tug at her clothes, the sun that followed each cloud was warm on her upturned face.

This time, when she concentrated on Hal, reaching out with her mind until she began to sense his heart beating alongside hers, the sensation was much stronger. Once more, she could feel unnatural darkness. A sensation of cool rock and vast, hollow proportions and a ceiling covered with long distorted pillars like stalactites. Turning to face the direction from which he drew her, she opened her eyes. She felt tiny shivers of gratitude course through her at the strength of the connection. She had driven too far once more, but this time she knew he was near and she was going to find him.

Hal had to be in some kind of cave, Grace thought as she drove slowly back the way she had come. The problem was that, as far as she knew, there were no caves in this part of Yorkshire. She had lived here all her life, and the only caves she had heard of were in the Yorkshire Dales, over an hour's drive from here. She decided to stop at the Sutton Bank visitor centre and ask if anyone there could help her. As soon as she turned into the car park her heart lifted. There were hardly any visitors at that time, and her little red Volkswagen Beetle was one of only three parked there. Trembling slightly with hopeful expectation, she pulled up next to it and ran across to the entrance, pulling open the heavy doors with such force that the pleasant-faced woman behind the information desk looked up with surprise.

'My car …. in your car park,' panted Grace.

The woman's face lit up. 'Ah, so that's yours! We were wondering about it — we noticed it first thing this morning and realised it must have been there all night.'

Grace felt a renewed sense of anxiety. 'My — my boyfriend was driving it — and I haven't been able to contact him since yesterday morning. I'm really afraid he's had some sort of accident. Are there any caves or pot-holes in the area?'

The woman looked perplexed. 'Not here, dear,' she answered, shaking her head. Grace felt bitter tears welling behind her eyes. She was close to Hal, she knew, but what could her vision have meant if not a cave? The kindly lady was really worried now, and called out to her colleague who had been straightening brochures at the far end of the room.

'Brian, this young lady is looking for her boyfriend — gone missing and left that red Beetle in the car park since yesterday. She thinks he may be lost in a cave near here. Can you think of anywhere?'

The man rubbed his beard thoughtfully as he walked toward them, slowly shaking his head.

'Caves, no, not near here. There are the old jet mines —' He broke off as he saw Grace's expression, and appeared uncomfortable at her distress. Suddenly his eyes brightened and he reached behind the desk for a ring-bound folder. Then he shuffled through the pages until he found what he had been looking for.

'All I can think of, lass, are the windypits,' he said, showing her a small article with a rather smudged black and white photo; a cluster of bones in a dark tunnel.

'There are quite a few of those here that are gradually being explored. There is evidence that they were used, maybe inhabited, as early as the Neolithic period. This one here', he indicated the grainy photo, 'the Slip Gill Windypit, had these bodies in it and the archaeologists think maybe they were murdered.'

Grace peered closely at the photo where she could just about see the grooves across the skull that the man was pointing to. Repugnant as the image was, it was not the same skull that Grace had seem in her dreams. However, she was sure she was on the right track now, Further probing revealed that there were over forty windypits in the area, and new ones were always being discovered.

'But we should get a proper search party out if you're that worried, lass,' said Brian, reluctantly interrupting his own discourse.

'Yes … all right,' said Grace. 'You do that. But I'm going to look for him now, myself, anyway.'

'No, listen, lass,' said Brian. 'You've got no chance on your own and it can be wild out there.'

'I can,' insisted Grace. 'I can't explain it. I've got this sort of …*sense.* It will lead me to him, I know it.'

'June, you talk to her,' said Brian in despair.

June folded her arms and glared at Brian to shut him up. Then she came over and put an arm around Grace. 'Now, you listen, lovey,' she said kindly. 'You go and look for him if you want, but you must keep in touch. Leave us your mobile number, and take the number here. We'll get in touch with Mountain Rescue for you — leave us both your names and a photo of him if you've got one. If you find him first and he's hurt' — here Grace gave a sob — 'I'm only saying *if* ... then they'll be able to get him to hospital faster than you can.'

Grace had to admit the sense of this and all the necessary details were exchanged before she rushed out to the Land Rover, feeling enormously relieved at finding a real clue to Hal's whereabouts at last. The couple had not seemed to find anything funny in the name *windypit* and Grace had forced herself to keep a straight face too. Now she burst out laughing. Trust Hal to fall down such an oddly named hole — and manage to make her laugh even when she was so worried!

A gentle rain began to fall as she walked, stopping now and then to get her bearings. She buttoned her cardigan up to the neck, wishing she had thought to bring a rain jacket. She followed the path until she saw the dark waters of Lake Gormire, and then stopped to feel the direction again. Left, she decided, and looked for a way down into the woods along the hill that led to Whitestone Cliff. Finally she found it, a narrow pathway that cut sharply down the steep escarpment. Her shoulders were already quite damp and she was glad of the thick canopy of leaves here that sheltered her from the rain somewhat. The path was unbelievably beautiful, and under other circumstances Grace would have been spellbound by the descent through silver birch, ash and oak, rain-slick branches interlacing in intricate patterns. The path wound down and down, interrupted now and then by gnarled tree roots or rough stones, slippery from the rain. Huge, moss-covered boulders studded the slope, reminders of old rock-falls from the cliffs above. Small plants and wildflowers flourished along the side, and goldfinches dipped and soared from branch to branch as they searched for a dry perch. A small sign near the bottom of the slope informed visitors that they were entering Garbutt Wood Nature Reserve. The massive trees here seemed ancient, prickly holly and saplings growing amongst the oaks. Grace stopped once more and reached out with her mind to Hal. The path led straight on toward the lake, but she felt drawn to the right, so she reluctantly abandoned the path and began pushing through the thick undergrowth.

Mindful of the possibility of those undiscovered windypits out there, Grace walked slowly and kept her eyes on the ground. Brian had said that several of the pits were up to thirty metres deep with multiple rifts that took hours to explore and which, formed by land slippage as most of them were, were pretty unstable. These thoughts were enough to subdue her spirits again. She began to fret about the state she would find Hal in, and how she would manage to reach him if he were buried so deep underground. Brushing at cobwebs that clung to her face, and grimacing as each young sapling she pushed past sent a cool shower of raindrops over her, she carried on until she reached a clearing.

A pungent scent of wet earth, fern and bracken was strong here, along with the exotic scent of gorse. Grace breathed deeply, looking round to get her bearings, and that was when she noticed the white of Hal's gym shoes protruding from one side of a huge gorse bush.

Grace ran across the clearing, oblivious to the rain or the risk of holes. Hal lay so still that dread filled her heart, and she found herself murmuring his name in an incoherent prayer. Rounding the bush she fell to her knees and stared at Hal, automatically taking stock of his visible injuries. He was covered in dirt and scratches and there was a nasty half-scabbed bump on his forehead. She reached out her hand and gently brushed his grimy blonde hair from his face.

'Aaah,' he yelped, sitting up in shock; then his blue gaze met hers and a small smile curved his mouth.

'Christ, Grace, you almost gave me a heart attack, creeping up on me like that,' he said, pulling her into his arms and cradling her close. He smelt odd, of sweat and blood and mud, and the waterproof jacket crackling beneath her face was soaked through — but he was safe. She lifted her head and kissed him gently, then laid her head back on his chest and let her tears of relief mingle with the rain.

21
The Order of the Dogs Templar

Hal had never felt so weak. He had been lying next to the gorse that had ripped him to shreds as he climbed from the windypit, relishing the relief at having escaped his underground prison, but also filled with an underlying sadness at the thought that his erstwhile friend, the ghost, had met a very different fate. The downpour drumming over him, and the melody of birdsong, dripping rain and whispering leaves had been the sweetest sounds he had ever heard. He had been completely unaware of Grace's presence until she had touched him, and the shock had almost finished him off but then, as his arms closed around her, he had felt his heart expand with joy.

His momentary bliss had lasted as long as it had taken for him to stand up and walk a few steps. Without the adrenalin that had coursed through his body and kept him going through the dark tunnels and the precipitous passage to freedom, his limbs felt like jelly. Fortunately, the storm front was heading away from them toward the sea, the distant flashes of lightning and rolling thunder a dramatic backdrop to their trek. The rain was quite enough to make the journey treacherous, and he had needed to rest frequently. It had taken ages for them to climb back up the escarpment, and by the time they reached the car park, soaked and shaking, he had felt quite ill and had made no fuss when Grace had insisted on taking him to Whitby hospital.

The journey there, with Grace driving Charlie's Land Rover, looking incongruously tiny behind the steering wheel, had passed in a blur. He had tried to make conversation, but his tongue felt thick and clumsy and his eyes too heavy to keep open, so he had settled for listening to her as she chatted on; she'd sensed him falling, knew he was in trouble ... so the next day she'd phoned his sister who had driven up and was staying on the boat ... she had slept in Grandma Clair's bed, too scared to be alone ... she had searched all their special places. Grace's voice had blended into the whirr of the heating fan that she had turned on to try to dry their clothes out and he had dozed off, feeling warmly contented.

***

Hal had managed to walk into the hospital under his own steam, but had then surrendered gladly to the ministrations of doctors and nurses. He had explained what had happened to him, but kept the bit about his ghostly helper to himself. When the doctor had decided to keep him in hospital overnight to make sure that he was not suffering from concussion, Hal was glad that he had not mentioned the voice, since he suspected they would have insisted on getting him psychiatric assistance too if he had told them everything.

As it was, he was now tucked up in the small men's ward. The other four beds were empty, for which he was extremely grateful, as the effort to make conversation would have been too much. He had been cleaned up, his scratches medicated and his chest X-rayed, revealing no bones broken beneath the bruised ribs. His reflexes had been deemed quite satisfactory and the prognosis was that the doctor would most likely discharge him after breakfast the next day.

Grace had pulled up a chair by his bed and sat holding his hand for a while, her beautiful face glowing with happiness and relief, until his eyes had begun to close against his will.

'Get some rest, darling,' she told him, kissing his forehead gently. 'You will need your strength to tell everyone all about your adventure. Grandma Clair will want to hear every detail, and Angelina and Leonardo are driving back from Roseberry Topping where they had gone to look for you.'

'Mr Marconi? What is *he* doing here?' Hal asked, and Grace shrugged her shoulders and suggested that maybe his sister had wanted company because she had been worried about him. Hal had noticed a quick flash of humour in Grace's eyes that he did not quite understand, but he had been too tired to ask anything else and had spent the next few hours sleeping, in spite of the brightness of the ward lights. He had been untroubled by dreams or nightmares, and woke when dinner was brought round just after 6pm. Grace had gone, as visitors were apparently now sent out of wards during mealtimes, and he missed her presence. He had felt her hand in his even while sleeping and thought that he never again wanted to be apart from her.

Hal found that he was ravenously hungry and attacked the bland white mess of chicken breast and mashed potato with more enthusiasm than he imagined the catering assistant had ever seen, wiping up the last bits with his bread roll before leaning back, replete at last. Feeling much better, he began to look forward to welcoming his visitors, although he was still not sure how much of his story to tell.

***

Grandma Clair shut the cage door on Thatcher, ignoring his whistles and screeches of protest. She put on her best cardigan, a soft, dusky pink cashmere which had been a present from Grace. Then she wrapped the multi-coloured scarf that she had finished knitting that afternoon around her neck, and picked up a plastic bag by the door that held a rich chocolate cake to tempt Hal's appetite. Not that the boy ever needed tempting! It was very satisfying to cook for Hal, whose appetite was gratifyingly formidable. Her husband had been the same and she missed having a man to cook for every day.

Outside, the unpredictable British weather lived up to its reputation. The storm had passed and swept the clouds out to sea, leaving the early evening sky bright and clear. The air was quite warm as she puffed uphill toward the hospital, and Clair reluctantly removed her scarf. It was a pity not to wear it, the colours were so pretty, and she wanted to make a good impression on Hal's sister, who sounded a rather stylish sort. Still, it did not matter, she was wearing her best purple-silk blouse and red wool skirt under the cardigan, so she would look nice anyway.

***

Angelina and Leo, walking up the same hill a few minutes later, were oblivious to everyone around them. Their attention was focussed on each other, aware of every brief touch of their hands. Grace's call, telling them that she had found Hal, had interrupted their passionate embrace in the summerhouse. When they had disentangled themselves they had found, to their surprise, that the storm had dissipated without their realising it. They had made their way back down Roseberry Topping, stopping frequently to kiss ardently, feeling like a pair of love-struck teenagers. In the car, Angelina had found a comb in her handbag and managed to restore some order to her hair, but after its soaking and without the benefit of hairdryer, it now kinked in odd directions. Her clothes were almost dry again and she had brushed most of the dirt from them, but she looked nothing like her usual elegant self. She was quite flushed, both with happiness over Hal's safe return, and a kind of embarrassed delight in the new-found tender spot in her heart. One look at the soppy expression on Leonardo's face was enough to prove he felt the same. Even now, walking separately through the busy streets, each was aware of a novel lightness of heart that they were trying, very ineffectively, to hide.

***

When the ward opened again after dinner, Hal was relieved to see that Grace was alone. He interrupted her as she began to speak, taking her hand and urging her to sit and listen. He had to tell her something that would sound pretty weird, but he wanted to do it before Angelina got there as he was not at all sure that he could talk about everything to anyone else. He had got no further than the first appearance of the ghostly voice in the windypit when Grandma Clair wheezed in, and after she had clasped him to her abundant bosom, lovingly squeezed his cheek and presented him with a wonderful smelling cake, Hal carried on with his tale. He didn't mind the old lady hearing about his experience. If there was anyone in the world who would not think he was mad, it was her. He rushed through his story and had just got to the part where the ghost might have given him a foot up to the ledge when he heard Angelina's voice in the corridor. Feeling quite out of breath, he collapsed against the pillows and looked expectantly toward the door.

Grace and her grandma exchanged eloquent looks across his bed as introductions were made all round. Hal held back his laughter as he saw Angelina taking in Grandma Clair's colourful appearance, although she did not look quite herself either, he thought. Her grey hair was ruffled untidily at the back and there were streaks of dirt on her jeans.

'We got caught in the storm,' she said coolly, seeing the direction of his gaze, then leant over to kiss him and tenderly ruffled his hair, making sure to avoid his bump. Leonardo shook hands with Hal and said how delighted he was to find him safe.

'We have had quite an extraordinary adventure,' he declared with a wry smile, making it sound as if the adventure had been his, and not Hal's. Oh well, Hal thought, his English could not be perfect *all* the time.

'So, what happened this time?' Angelina asked, raising a dark brow.

'I fell down a windypit, Lili,' Hal began — and then waited patiently for the general laughter this statement provoked to die down before retelling his carefully edited tale. He did mention the skeleton, and was rewarded by murmurs of horror at the thought of spending the night with such a macabre companion.

Although he did not want to talk much about the ghostly company he had shared in the pits, he could not refrain from mentioning it completely.

'It was an odd sensation,' he admitted. 'There were moments when I felt that I was not alone down there. At times I even thought that I could hear another voice ...,' he tailed off and was surprised when Leonardo nodded knowingly at him.

'Since my near-death experience I have sometimes felt a strange presence myself,' he said with a wary look at Angelina. She did not appear to have heard, though, her maternal instinct having been aroused again at Hal's confession.

Frowning at him, she held out a hand, touching his forehead to gauge his temperature and exclaimed, 'That sounds like a hallucination to me, Hal! Maybe you do have a bit of concussion after all. I think it is a good job they are keeping you here tonight.'

Looking into the faces surrounding him, full of love and friendship, Hal felt lucky to be alive. Grandma Clair was missing from the circle around the bed, and he caught glimpses of her as she pottered around, straightening chairs near the empty beds, brushing down his dirty clothes which she had found in the bedside locker. She paid particular attention to his jeans, smoothing them out and laying then across the Formica top of the locker. She left enough space for her chocolate cake, which she then sliced with the knife she had thought to bring, and offered it round to everyone.

Angelina and Leonardo each took a large slice and munched with enthusiasm, explaining that they had not eaten since breakfast.

'You must come on home with me. I have a nice stew that I prepared earlier,' Grandma Clair said at once with an odd twinkle in her eyes; but she did not seem surprised or disappointed when Angelina graciously declined, saying that she was very tired. Hal did not think that she *looked* tired — but maybe that was the relief at finding him in one piece. Leonardo backed her up but avoided looking at her, which Hal found a little strange. There seemed to be a bit of tension in the air between them. Maybe they had argued and did not want to have to spend an evening being polite to each other? Knowing his sister, Hal thought that seemed all too probable.

Grandma Clair exchanged another knowing look with Grace.

'You get a good night's rest now. Don't you worry about things, just get yourself well again.' Enfolded in the old lady's ample padding, Hal tried to nod. 'Gracie will stay with you a while longer, I'm sure but I must get back to Thatcher or he will not speak to me all night.' She released him, gave Grace a kiss and alarmed Angelina by pulling her down and hugging her hard. Leonardo avoided a similar embrace by kissing the old lady's hand in a very gallant gesture which made her chuckle. They could hear her wheezing with laughter as she trundled off along the corridor.

'Thatcher?' Angelina asked, and listened with a bemused smile as Grace and Hal took it in turn to describe Grandma Clair's feathered friend.

Grace perched on the bed next to Hal, stroking his hair absentmindedly, and he placed his hand on her warm thigh, contentedly absorbing her nearness. Scratches from his tangle with the gorse bush decorated both backs and palms of his hands, and throbbed a bit too, but with Grace so close he did not care. He caught Leonardo's eye and was pleased to see him wink. Taking Angelina gently by the arm, he suggested that they leave Hal to get some rest. To Hal's surprise, his sister readily agreed. She gave him a light kiss, smiled warmly at Grace, and then waited for Leonardo to say his own goodbyes, watching him with a curious look that Hal did not recognise.

When they were alone again, Hal pulled Grace closer and she kicked off her shoes and snuggled into him. Hal kissed her hair, breathing in the sweet scent of rain-drenched leaves that clung there.

'About that ghost I saw —'

'Don't worry about it, Hal. Grandma Clair sees them all the time and although I don't see or hear spirits, I have my own peculiarities — as you know.' She looked up at him, laughing, and Hal was so grateful in that moment to be alive, here, with her in his arms that he felt he could burst with joy.

'I think that there are some places that absorb the essence of those who lived there. Certainly there is more to life than what we can see and touch in the physical world.'

'I'm not worried really, although before, if anyone had told me I would be chatting to a dead man, I would have said it was impossible. You know I adore your Grandma, but I've always thought she was a harmless old crackpot — and I have to admit that I never really took your own *feelings* very seriously,'

'I know.' Grace did not seem annoyed at his confession, but Hal felt chagrined anyway. He had always put Grace's psychic abilities down to an over-active imagination, and it was only now that he realised how patient she had been with him. He had been a fool, he realised, shoving his hair off his forehead and wincing as his fingers caught the bump that he had momentarily forgotten about. He felt different tonight. His vigil in the caves had allowed him to look deep into himself. Certain things he had liked, others he had determined to change.

'I learnt a bit about myself down there, I reckon. Saw a few truths that needed facing up to. But maybe the most important thing I found was when the voice talked about everyone searching for their own Holy Grail _ whatever that is. I guess it is different things for different people. He talked about learning to love, without judgement, which of course is what you have been saying ever since we met!' Grace's laugh was like liquid honey that rolled through him, warming his soul.

'So, Sir Hal, have you found your Grail?' she teased. Hal knew that he had, and was cuddling it right now.

'Unconditional love ...' he muttered, slightly breathless as Grace's fingers traced the shape of his chest beneath the hospital gown. He trapped her fingers, casting a glance at the doorway in case one of the scarily efficient nurses should pass by. Then a thought struck him and he snorted, 'I suppose that all dogs must be true knights then. They know how to love unconditionally all right. The Order of the Dogs Templar!'

Grace seemed far less worried about the nurses, maybe because she had not had them sticking needles into her or plumping up pillows with unnecessary force. She gave a little *woof* and bit his ear gently. Pushing her away and restoring his dignity, Hal changed the subject.

'Was it my imagination, or was Lili behaving oddly?' he asked.

'Well, I don't really know her, so I wouldn't know what was odd for her, but she didn't seem strange to me. Oddness does run in the family, of course,' she teased — and squealed as Hal tickled her in revenge.

'Cheek! Thank goodness. You were all being so nice to me before that I was worried that I must really look bad. About Lili, though, I have never seen her look so uncoordinated ... she looked different for some reason, younger and almost pretty.'

'Love tends to have that effect,' Grace said, sliding down in his arms and kissing him sensuously. This time

Hal returned her kiss with enthusiasm, then pulled away, looking enquiringly into her laughing eyes.

'What – Lili and Mr Marconi?'

'Why not?'

'Why not, indeed.' Hal laughed too, finding the idea of his uptight sister and the urbane Italian too funny for words. Then he concentrated on finishing the kiss properly and found that it was all too possible to get overheated, concussion or not.

Grace broke away and climbed off the bed, giggling as she smoothed her clothes down and took up a more decorous position on the bedside chair. She regarded him with a mock stern look on her flushed face. Head tilted to one side questioningly, she cleared her throat.

'Hal Snow, what is it that you want to say? Obviously you're itching to get something out.' Her voice was deep and husky. He should have known that he could not keep a secret from Grace. She saw through him completely. He remembered the ring in his jeans pocket and gave a smug little smile. Grace was not the only one who could read his mind and knew what he needed, he realised. That was what Grandma Clair had been doing earlier when she had been bustling around the room, reorganising stuff: she must have felt the ring pouch in his pocket and been unable to resist seeing what it contained. Then she had made sure he had his jeans close at hand. Gratefully, he reached behind Grace, slipped his fingers into the pocket and drew out the small pouch, then hesitated.

'Grace darling, I thought about this so much down in the windypit. I promised myself that if I got out I would ask you as soon as I could. I wanted this to be such a perfect, romantic moment, but this hardly seems the right place or time.'

'It is *exactly* right,' Grace replied.

'Grace, darling. Please, please will you do me the enormous honour of marrying me?'

Grace said nothing, but her eyes glistened with sudden tears, and she wordlessly held out her left hand. Hal took her fine-boned hand in his, and with slightly trembling fingers slid the ring onto her index finger. Under the harsh lights of the ward, the little diamonds around the emerald shot sparks across the smooth brown skin of her arm, and Hal realised that Grace was absolutely right. There could be no better moment than this.

22

The Ghost and Grandma Clair

Grandma Clair finished her stew and wiped a small piece of bread in the gravy before putting it onto Thatcher's saucer. He deserved a little treat for being shut up in his cage for so long that afternoon, she thought, nodding at the bright-eyed bird and confirming that he was indeed a very pretty boy. Leaving him pecking daintily at the bread, she began to wash up the dinner things, taking up her narrative again as she informed Grandpa Jimmy about the day's events. She had already shared most of Hal's adventure and told him about how happy the young ones had looked and about the ring she had found in Hal's jeans. Now she regaled him with her other impressions of the evening, casting meaningful glances toward the empty chair at the head of the table.

"Jimmy, you should have seen that sister of Hal's. Hal told us about her at dinner that time, do you remember? Well, she was almost as tall as him with big, sharp bones and she looked all cool and icy when she came in until she saw Hal. I could tell how much she loved him then. You would have liked her, you always did like a long-legged woman. She was not as immaculate as I had imagined, though. She had dirt all over her trousers. So did that charming Mr Marconi!"

Grandma Clair laughed so hard at the idea of those too together that she had to sit down again. Thatcher chirped merrily and hopped onto her shoulder where he nibbled her ear lobe affectionately.

"Hal will be alright. He has nothing worse than a few bruises and scratches but he sure got a fright in those windypits. He met a spirit down there and now he's not sure if it really happened or if he maybe made it all up ... Some folks just don't understand, do they my dear?" She lovingly patted the invisible hand on the table, shaking her head at the idea that other people could be oblivious of the spirit world.

She shook a few seeds from Thatcher's food tin into her hand and showed them to him then heaved herself up and went into the lounge where she tempted the bird into his cage for the second time that day. Covering the cage with an old shawl she kept for that purpose, she chatted to Thatcher for a while until he stopped grumbling and settled for the night. He was a good bird but there were times when she did not want to be interrupted at inappropriate moments. Grandma Clair moved around the small room, lighting candles that were dotted here and there then turning off the main light so that the room was illuminated in a warm, flickering glow.

"Good night Jimmy dear," she dismissed her husband's spirit with a tender smile and sank onto the comfy old sofa. Pulling the coffee table closer, she rummaged in her cardigan pocket and pulled out the small piece of rock that she had taken from Hal's jacket pocket at the hospital. The rock felt cold and rough in her hand. She placed it in front of her on the table and looked at it curiously. It was a pretty unappealing thing as crystals go, a dull, creamy-coloured lump. However, she knew from experience that it would contain the essence of the spirit that had dwelled close to it for so many years.

She had been very moved by Hal's tale. Whilst Grace had been concerned only with the safety of her beloved, Grandma Clair had felt touched by the plight of the ghost, condemned to eternity in a cold, dark cave by its need to make penance for its unconfessed sins. She let the air settle like a warm cloak around her, smiling to herself as she waited for total peace and when she felt ready she picked up the moonmilk and settled herself more comfortably among the soft cushions, then closed her eyes.

Slowly, out of the darkness behind her eyelids an image formed. She did not see the skeleton at the base of the shaft that Hal had described but rather a vague shape that hovered just beyond her reach. Grandma Clair murmured softly, her personal litany of reassurance and compassion that she used to establish contact with troubled visitors to her mind. After a while she sensed a change as the spirit became aware of her too.

A weary, white-bearded face. Sparse white hair tied behind his head. Gaunt cheek bones beneath surprisingly youthful eyes with a gentle look in their brown depths. Then a host of emotions, a storm of memories that shook her solid frame and made her gasp. Centuries of loneliness engulfed her.

She made the reassuring noises that she made when Thatcher was sulking in his cage, refusing to come out. She knew by now that nothing from the spirit world could hurt her, no matter how sad or violent the wounded soul might be. She reached out with her mind, sending relief, sympathy and her intrinsic warmth toward the old man.

"Would it help if I promise you a proper burial for your bones?" she wondered then laughed aloud as the spirit's voice cackled in her mind,

"A better burial than mine would be hard to arrange, methinks, but I thank thee for thy kindness."

Grandma Clair patted the sofa next to her invitingly and grinned. This promised to be an entertaining visit.

23

A Brave New Love

Angelina could not remember ever feeling quite so content. Leo had opened one of the bottles of wine he had brought, and quickly rustled up some thin wedges of cheese and a packet of salted crisps to munch on while they enjoyed their aperitif on deck. All signs of the storm had vanished as if it had never occurred, their mussed-up hair and slightly damp clothes the only reminder of its violence. Sipping the mellow, deep-red wine while the early evening sun burnished the rippling river, she felt a warmth inside that had only a little to do with the alcohol.

'How many bottles of this wine did you say you brought with you?'

'Only four — I was not sure how many days we might be away — but I thought four would probably be enough,'

'It's very good.' She hid her smile in the glass and took another sip. Leonardo Marconi might not be every woman's dream but with his thick hair standing up wildly and the setting sun stroking his curls and skin with gold, he looked just right to her.

'It comes from a quaint hill-town in Tuscany called Montalcino. I'd like to take you there one day…'

'Mmm, Montalcino,' she mused, meeting his gaze with a smile 'What a nice idea.' Life seemed incredibly good right then. Hal was safe and she had been relieved to find she liked his girlfriend very much. She had hoped she would, but had harboured a small concern that they might not be compatible. She liked the odd grandmother too. Most of all, she liked Mr Marconi.

The snack had served to make her hungrier than ever, and she half-heartedly mentioned cooking something. She did not feel like eating out, wanting to preserve this atmosphere of intimacy between them but neither did she feel like tackling Hal's spartan kitchen to unearth food and some decent pans.

'Let me have a shower first and then, while you are using all the rest of the water in the tanks, I can prepare something for us to eat. How does that sound?'

'Apart from that rude remark about the amount of water I use, it sounds absolutely marvellous', she told him with a smile. The smile grew bigger as she heard him singing loudly under the shower a few minutes later. He had a fine baritone voice that carried over the water and scared a few gulls away. He finished remarkably quickly. He had been quite right to go first. Angelina needed time to pamper herself and dry her hair properly.

Hal's rules be damned! She no longer had any doubts about whether or not Leo found her attractive, but it would not do any harm to make herself look as good as possible for him. She was pondering what to wear when she heard the bathroom door open and looked through the hatch to see a brief glimpse of Leonardo, wearing nothing but a small towel around his waist, before he disappeared into the cabin. Angelina was instantly reminded of the funny dream she had had days ago, of a bare-chested Mr Marconi dressed as a sheikh. He might be slightly pigeon-chested, but his skin was an attractive golden brown, a legacy of the Roman weather.

Her euphoric mood vanished as she entered the tiny bathroom. Leonardo had helpfully left the sink pulled out above the toilet, and the now damp wood stuck when she tried to shove it back in. If she broke something Hal would not be pleased, so somehow she managed to squeeze into the space between toilet and sink and relieve her bladder. That urgent task out of the way, she had to remember just which switch by the side of the toilet directed the contents to the holding tank and which would pump river water into the bowl. By the time she had finished all that she still had to try to shower, standing on the slatted wooden floor that marked the right spot, without splashing the rest of the room too much. Obviously that was impossible, so she spent a few minutes after her shower wiping down all the surfaces. Then she tried to look at her face in the mirror. It was the perfect height for her face, but too small to see anything else, and the age-mottled surface was very unforgiving. With her large toiletry bag now wedged in the sink, she applied body lotion and then yanked a leg up to rest on the sink rim while she painted her toe nails.

Exhausted after these acrobatics, she rummaged in Hal's cupboard for the travel hairdryer she had left there on her first visit to *Calypso*. It had clearly never been used by Hal, and she eventually located it behind a row of toilet paper. Then she found there was no adapter plug, which the hairdryer needed to connect to the boat's 12-volt electrical system. Seething, she opened the door a fraction and called out to ask Leo if he could locate one. He found one remarkably quickly and passed it to her through the gap in the door with a chuckle. Remembering Leo's enthusiastic remarks about the practicability of the head the previous night, Angelina sniffed loudly. While the noise of the hairdryer covered her voice, she freely gave vent to her opinions about men and bathrooms.

Some time later — quite a lot of time if she were truthful — Angelina joined Leo in the galley, feeling clean and restored. He looked up at her as she brushed past him, and gave a low whistle of appreciation. She had applied a little perfume and added mascara and soft pink lipstick. Deciding what to wear had been a challenge as she had nothing special that would look right without her trademark high heels. Eventually she had settled for her black linen trousers and a dusky-lavender top made of silk-jersey that draped softly over her body, giving at least the *impression* of curves. She had left her feet bare apart from the pale pink nail varnish. Delicate pearl drops completed her simple but elegant look.

Leo was wearing his jeans, which he had given a good brush, and a clean navy-blue shirt. Of the yellow sweater there was, fortunately, no sign.

'What can I do?' she asked as he handed her a fresh glass of wine. He indicated a chopping board and got her to thinly slice a courgette. Leo looked so at home in the cramped galley. He had managed to find something melodious in amongst Hal's ghastly collection of heavy metal and groups she had never heard of, and a gentle Latin-American rhythm was playing in the background. Leo hummed along as he chopped onions and whisked eggs. He had set the table already, as it was too cold to sit out on deck by now. Inside it was quite balmy as Leonardo had also found Hal's small heater which worked a treat in the cramped space.

There was a bread basket and also a tempting plate with bits of toast topped with chopped tomatoes. Angelina picked one up and nibbled, tasting olive oil and pungent raw garlic mixed with the tomato.

'Marvellous!'

'*Crostini con pomodoro fresco e tanto aglio*, it sounds so much better than saying tomato with garlic, don't you agree, dear?'

'*Aglio.*' Angelina got her tongue around the unfamiliar word and smiled, feeding her last bite to Leo, then wiping an elusive bit of tomato from his chin with her finger.

'I will teach you Italian,' he promised, turning his attention to the frying pan, from which a wonderful scent of onions was emanating. Angelina sat at the table and watched Leo's back as he cooked. She studied the wine label and imagined Leo showing her around Italy and teaching her Italian. She looked up to find him studying her as intently as she had been looking at the bottle. His eyes were almost black in the dim light of the galley, and she felt her stomach lurch at the intensity of his gaze.

'This is Rosso di Montalcino which is a little lighter and fresher than the famous Brunello from that region,' he said as he touched his glass to hers, and they both sipped. Then he leant across the table and touched his lips to hers very softly, their first kiss since they had left Roseberry Topping, so full of promise that Angelina felt the heat rise up across her chest and neck.

Was it possible that only a few days before she had believed herself to be happily self-sufficient and completely hardened against romance? She had not known until now just how lonely she had been. With Leo by her side, his sardonic quips and cynical humour so akin to her own, she felt whole, as if she had found her missing other half. *You would never have known what you were missing if he had not insisted on accompanying you here*, she realised incredulously.

Leo finished the omelette he had been making and slid a thick wedge onto her plate.

'This is my speciality, a *frittata, con cipolle e zucchine,'* he informed her with a grin, spearing a piece with his fork and helping it into his mouth with a crust of bread in a gesture that was unmistakeably Italian.

The food was delicious, the wine was fruity and aromatic, and Angelina felt as if she were melting. It was as though the hard, icy core that she had built around herself since childhood was slowly melting away. She had been ravenous but now, after a few mouthfuls, all she could think of was the proximity of Leo and the way his eyes searched hers. She pushed her plate away.

'I think it is time we went to bed,' she declared, in a slightly breathless voice.

Leonardo's eyes twinkled and he picked up her hand and kissed her fingers saying, 'I could not agree more, madam!'

'I was wondering ...'

'Oh dear, should I be worried?'

'Probably! No, it is just that, in terms of bruising potential, do you think it would be better to make love here or retire to the cabin?' Leo laughed and declared that the cabin was undoubtedly more bruise-resistant, then sent her on ahead while he went to shut off the gas and close the hatches safely.

***

Leo watched Angelina until she closed the head door behind her, then took a final sip of wine and went on deck. It was slightly chilly but the sky was clear, and faint starlight showed through the glow from the town lights. He shut off the gas and crossed to the side rail, looking down into the dark water that eddied around *Calypso's* hull. Not so long ago he had stood looking into a different river with pain hammering his temples and death at his heels. Now it was his heart that was pounding, and he was certain that the only thing pursuing him tonight was love. He smiled to himself, going over the events of the day in his mind, replaying Angelina's caustic remarks that disguised her underlying warmth. Thoughts of her anxious face as she worried about Hal, hair plastered to her scalp and rain dripping from her sharp nose mingled with other, far more sensual memories.

Turning to go back into the warm cabin, Leo was brought up short. A few feet away, leaning against the mast, was his doppelganger. He had thought these images were a result of his aneurysm and had hoped that they would be a temporary blip on his sanity. He had empathised with Hal earlier when he had mentioned hearing voices, but at least Hal had not been *seeing* things. His vision looked back at him with his own morose and craggy face and drew deeply on a half-smoked cigarette. Riverweed clung wetly to his hair and clothes, and his expression was antagonistic.

'*So, what now? Do you think there is going to be some happy ending here? You of all people should know better. What do you see in her anyway? She's old –*

you're old, for Christ's sake! Have you looked at yourself in a mirror recently? What have you got to offer any woman? Take my advice, finish that wine, light yourself a cigarette, get on with ...'

Leonardo's attention was distracted from the diatribe by the sound of a door opening. He bent to look into the cabin just in time to see Angelina smile up at him, then turn her back. There was the delightful slithering sound of silk on smooth flesh. Her ivory nightdress plunged the full length of her back, held in place by fragile criss-crossing straps. She was long, pale and infinitely tempting.

Leo did not hesitate. He no longer needed anything else to fill his lonely heart.

'Be gone,' he told his old self simply, and turned his back on him completely. He was already half way down the steps when he heard a small splash. He smiled determinedly and reached for the hatch cover, letting Drowned Leo return forever to the watery bed from whence he had risen.

As he pulled the hatch firmly closed he heard a muffled yelp from the cabin and Angelina saying resignedly, 'I don't believe it, that will be another bruise tomorrow!'

'Where this time?' Leo inquired sympathetically.

'My thighs are black and blue,' she informed him sharply.

Imagining those long thighs made Leo feel almost giddy. How very wonderful it was to be alive! And now, he thought, he had better go and kiss it all better.

ABOUT THIS BOOK

This book started in a very different way to my others, with the death of a dear friend. The events in the first chapter were so very hard to write with a sense of humour, because the real life events did not have a happy ending. We will never know exactly what happened to Tony but he had suffered two aneurysms shortly before he disappeared from his boat on the Tevere River one day. His body was discovered ten days later near the mouth of the river, floating out to the sea he had so loved.

I found that I could not accept this tragic death and later, when I was searching for the perfect love-interest for a great new character I wanted to write about (Miss Angelina Snow), I found myself thinking about Tony so much that a small part of my character Leonardo Marconi is based on him. Of course the events and character in the book are completely fictitious but I like to think that I have given Leonardo the life that Tony *should* have had and that he would not have been too disapproving of my story. He is, and always will be, greatly missed.

All other characters in the book are completely fictitious, although I have to admit to using some of my son James' traits when describing Hal, in particular his taste in music!

People always ask me if I base my female characters on myself. The answer is no. In Angelina's case, she is marvellously tall and skinny while my height has been compared to that of a garden gnome, by some cheeky members of the family. I do have one trait in common with this formidable lady - I love shoes that make a loud noise as I stride along.

As always, I want to make it very clear that, unlike some of the relatives described in this story, my own parents are absolutely wonderful. They have always believed in me and showered me with love and affection. I am very proud to be their daughter.

My other books have been set in Italy, where we live most of the time. However, I love and miss England and this time wanted to write about the country I consider to be my soul place.

My parents used to live in Bourne, a lovely, friendly town in Lincolnshire which I wanted to use as the setting for some of the adventures. I also needed another location by the sea.

After viewing a great television program whilst on a short holiday in England, I dragged Guido off, in the middle of winter to visit Whitby. Guido loves the Italian summer sun and sailing in non-tidal waters but he gallantly accompanied me, driving us around the wonderful moorland and coastal villages of North Yorkshire. I gathered all the information I needed except for a cave, which one of my characters had to fall into. Unfortunately everyone I spoke to told me that the only caves nearby were in the Dales. We had no time to visit that area too and it was in desperation, in the middle of a snow storm, that I made Guido stop at the Sutton Bank information centre on our way back to Bourne. Here the helpful staff told me about the delightfully named Windy Pits. The name 'windypit' is thought to refer to the rising of warm or cold air from the fissures and of course, being very childish, it made me giggle and was just what I had been looking for. Many thanks to them for their help!

Calypso is based on our own beautiful boat *Euriklea*. Angelina is not the only one to dislike the cramped and spartan heads or suffer from bruises all over. However, unlike her, I absolutely loved living on our boat! Thanks to Gary Pearson, Assistant Harbour Master of Whitby and Scarborough Harbours for taking the time to make sure my details about mooring and sailing there were possible even though Whitby is not strictly a residential harbour.

My grandmother had a budgerigar called Timmy who used to sit on her knitting needles and make odd noises, so Thatcher's behaviour is quite authentic.

As to the ghostly apparitions in the book. I have never had any such encounter but know of many people who claim to have seen or felt unusual things, so who am I to disbelieve?

I can tell you that this book was a joy to write. It often made me giggle out loud and I hope that it made you smile too. I'd love to hear from you. My e-mail is at the end of the book, so get in touch.

Every effort has been taken to proofread this document carefully, however errors occasionally can slip through, so if you find any please let me know However, bear in mind that I am a British writer and use British spelling and grammar. This may sometimes differ from what US readers are accustomed to.

TONIA PARRONCHI

Tonia Parronchi was born and grew up in England,
where she obtained a degree in English Literature.
She then worked in the travel industry and in
fashion before moving to Italy in 1990.
She and her husband, Guido live most of the time
in Tuscany, which is the setting for her novel
'The Song of the Cypress.'
Her other book, also set in Italy, is a humorous
memoir of their family sailing adventures,
'A Whisper on the Mediterranean'.

Tonia loves to hear from her readers, so feel free to
contact her at toniaparronchiauthor@gmail.com and visit
her website www.toniaparronchi.com

Printed in Great Britain
by Amazon